Chapter One

Thousands of seasons of deciduous rot in the sandstone ridges of this Ohio valley yielded wheat fields that brought farmers begging to buy Brubaker land. My great-grandfather convinced a Brubaker to sell him three hundred acres, not revealing to anyone he had discovered a spring-fed patch of land. Land that would never go dry. So while our land never rivaled the Brubaker's in size, my great-grandfather made a name for the Connells. And names could last for generations.

In winter, this valley belonged to no one. Snow covered the fields and then drifted over our fences. I wrapped my scarf around my head and stepped into my boots on the black rubber mat by the door. The snow from last night's milking puddled between a row of boots that promised seasons to come: my mid-calf green rubber boots for spring, the tan suede hiking boots with yellow laces for summer.

Quickly lacing my boots, I worried Zela's daughter would wake before I returned from milking, or, worse, that Zela would arrive and find her alone. Zela had never left her only child in my care. Most women assumed I had no instinct at all if I didn't have the sense to marry and give birth to my own children.

Reaching for my thermos on the kitchen counter, I noticed a neatly stacked pile of cloth next to the telephone. I flicked on the light. Zela's aprons. Starched and pressed. This was the second time Zela had left her aprons at my house. Yet she knew I would never use them. Cooking could not stain my work clothes any more than transmission oil, so I never bothered.

In November when she first left these aprons, I folded them over a hanger and kept them near the door, hoping to prompt her to explain why she hadn't simply tucked them in a drawer or donated them to her church's rummage sale. Only a month later, she slipped in the side door quietly. By the time I came into the hallway, her coat bulged slightly from the aprons tucked inside. Her silence encouraged my silence. If I noticed her taking them, she didn't want me to mention it.

"What does he say to make you stop wearing aprons, and then make you start wearing them again?" I asked.

Zela rubbed her hands on her legs as if she already wore an apron that could absorb the nervousness in her palms. I knew she wouldn't answer. Our friendship was based on old secrets, not new ones.

"I changed my mind. Look at this one." She took an apron from her purse. It was imprinted with small Jersey cows, causing her to laugh more with her mouth than her eyes. "How could I stop wearing this?"

"You always have a place here."

Zela's smile snapped off as quickly as she had snapped it on. No one defended a man better than a woman defending him to herself. Zela seemed to love Nathaniel most when I implied what I really thought of him.

"He's a good man, Dottie," she said. "He takes care of Mattie and me. Think of where I'd be without him." Then she hesitated.

"Here," I said for her. "You'd be stuck in the valley."

Zela had always known she would marry and move to doctors' row in Mansfield as I had always known I would farm my father's land and pay a debt he should not have owed. One could say we both succeeded.

In our twenties, Zela still talked about my living alone in this valley, because we both believed it would change. But when my farm hands stopped winking at me and started calling me ma'am, I knew something had passed me by. As I neared my forties, I made little effort to remain attractive. The random freckles on my forehead and cheeks darkened from working outdoors. My face always looked flushed, whether from sunburn, windburn, or exertion. Work had carved its designs on my body, stocky from eating well and sturdy from relying on my own strength.

Yet my appearance was not the only reason farm hands called me ma'am. I had become too accustomed to carrying myself as one already spoken for. Men expected me to say no. Zela had not teased me in years for having men work for me. And I would not ask her why she used aprons to hint at conversations she wouldn't have.

Snow covered the path to the barn. Few of us in the valley kept animals, but I kept three cows because I hated empty barns and slow winters. I sold the excess milk to neighbors whose barns housed International Harvesters instead of Holsteins. Zela must have known I would leave Mattie asleep and alone come milking time. Yet Zela had left before I thought to ask.

The night before, as I ate stewed tomatoes from a jar and worked on my crossword puzzle, Zela rang the doorbell. Those who knew me well enough to drive down my lane knocked, so I opened the door expecting a stranger. But there stood Zela with Mattie holding her mother's hand between both her hands as if she might slip. Zela did not seem to notice me until I asked, "What are you ringing the bell for?"

Zela was not one to ask favors. So when she asked us to give her a few moments alone in the sitting room, I asked Mattie to help me make supper. Mattie interrupted the cadenced work ethic I had inherited from my mother, who had worked to an unseen metronome as she thrust a shirt along the washboard. With Mattie, I could not attain this rhythm as I chopped potatoes and beets to prepare a small meal for them. She pestered me with questions about where I kept my television, why I lived alone, why I did not eat supper with my hired man. Mattie had Zela's tight-lipped smile, which could convey pleasure or disdain. As with Zela, I found myself smiling more, hoping to draw out of her a real smile, one I could trust. Eventually I went to the sitting room to tell Zela I didn't know how to occupy an eight-year-old.

Zela sat in the dark. I paused before flipping the light switch. The sitting room had always made Zela prefer my mother to hers and made me prefer Zela's mother to mine. After giving up on me, my mother decorated the room the way her Victorian mother had dressed her. Over the windows, she hung lace I would have shredded climbing my oak tree. She covered a chair in fabric too fine to sit on, let alone dress up a daughter prone to wading through the creek.

Zela sat on this chair that I had neither the time nor money to replace. I hesitated at the sight of my childhood friend staring at the farm that once belonged to her family. The brick two-story Brubaker home still stood, though it was now owned by Zela's distant relative. Unlike other farms in the seven-mile stretch of Maplewood Valley, our farmhouses shared a curve in the road.

The sharp right-hand turns and steep hills hid the other farms from view of one another, so it seemed that one's small nook in the valley was all that God created.

"Men should have to work with their hands," Zela said suddenly without turning to face me. "Makes them better men."

I waited, stiffening as if I'd approached a horse too quickly from behind; any sudden movement could frighten her and cause her to run off.

Then she said, "I need to leave Mattie here tonight."

I wished now that I asked her why, though when Zela slipped out the side door without telling us good-bye, I didn't worry. Our friendship stood on an understanding that sometimes it was better to let someone be.

Zela still had not come by the time I finished the milking, and the spare room was still dark, so I considered walking as I did every winter morning. Mattie would not have brought clothes warm enough to join me.

Folks in the valley coped with winter in their own way. Evelyn volunteered at the hospital. The Goswells and the Russells had fierce euchre competitions. The cold created an instinctual desire for warmth that sent Retha into a knitting fit that could outfit the valley in mittens by February. I felt lonelier at night, and night lasted longer in the winter. Winter nights could make me forget why I gave up everything to farm this land. Walking my back forty acres helped me remember. Though I had cleared many acres, the back forty had been my first. I had mined the limestone rocks and tilled the new field's virgin soil, thick with humus, abundant with earthworms.

As I walked past the heated machine shed, I heard the telephone ringing. I waited a moment to see if Stanley, my hired hand, would answer it. He had spent the last few days in the shed fiddling with a dying carburetor. After the phone rang a third time, I remembered asking him to tap a few maples. I jiggled the shed handle, pockmarked with rust.

The shed's warmth seeped between my long underwear, T-shirt, and turtleneck. I worked off my jacket while picking up the phone. My hello, gruff from the cold, startled someone on the other end.

"Sorry to interrupt your milking, Dottie."

It took me a moment to place the voice of Garret Hamilton. He was still called "Champ" more often than "Chief." None of his efforts in law enforcement had surpassed his winning shot in the basketball state championship in '39. Even his clout as police chief seemed to rest on that shot.

"Check your watch, Champ. I finished a while ago."

With a few cows of his own, he should have known this. A slow cool settled on my shoulders like an evening dusting of snow.

"Have you talked to Zela recently?"

"Sure, she came over last night."

"We're looking for Mattie. Did Zela mention leaving her with someone?"

Dread coursed through me like blood into a hand numbed from awkward sleep. I felt terribly alive. "She's here with me."

His voice was muffled as if he'd covered the receiver. He sounded relieved, and I exhaled, realizing I had held my breath.

"Should have tried you earlier," he said. "Her Uncle Morris was convinced she was visiting a friend in town."

"Why couldn't you ask her?" I paused and asked again, "Why couldn't you ask Zela?" as if the question could delay the answer.

"Dottie, there was a fire."

And then he told me what he knew. I heard little and remembered less. I only knew at the end of the conversation that a shell of the house remained, and Zela and Nathaniel had not made it out.

I wished at that moment that Morris had called instead. I had never experienced death without him, and the ache sank faster into my bones. Even though we had not spoken in seventeen years, I wanted him to sit with me next to Mattie. We would wait quietly until she woke, agreeing by our silence to give her a gift she would never know we had given.

When she stirred, he would hold me as I held her. I would tell her simply what happened without any details, because details carved pockets for the pain to settle into and take root.

I slowly slid to the ground and wrapped my arms around my knees. "Zela," I whispered.

The sharp clang of a bell echoed a hollow imitation across the fields. The pattern brought comfort until I realized it was my dinner bell. I ran out of the shed, leaving my coat on the nail. Mattie stood on the picnic table on the porch, leaning over to reach the knotted rope. I had shown her the bell two summers earlier and had told her how my mother called us back to the house by ringing it. Mattie's bare feet were planted in the mound of snow covering the table. She looked frightened. Nothing I said that day diminished that expression.

The Mansfield Journal ran the story on the front page with photographs of the neighbors holding their children wrapped in blankets as they watched the house crumble. Zela's neighbors rushed onto their front lawns at three in the morning. By then the roof had already collapsed. The firemen came to contain the fire, not to save the two-story brownstone that dripped fiery green awnings like melting icicles. A child in the photograph gazed at the sight with awe. The story quoted Chief Hamilton repeating what he said to me when he learned Mattie was alive. "Mothers have a mighty powerful intuition." I wondered if he believed it either time.

Chapter Two

As a child Zela preferred her ice cream "all dressed up," as she liked to say, so on Saturday afternoons we left my mother at the dry goods store and walked to Palmer's Drug Store to get Zela's ice cream with extra caramel, chocolate, chopped peanuts, and cherries for the same price as a vanilla cone at Shelton's Soda Shop.

Mr. Palmer competed single-handedly with every store in town by adding new aisles and products. After the soda shop opened, he built a counter with four stools and two booths in the back corner of his shop. He left the ice cream scooping to his teenage son Boyd, who paid little attention to anyone's order for one or two scoops. He wielded the ice cream scoop like a backhoe, pressing whatever he extracted into a glass dish. Mr. Palmer had little time to notice the extravagance. Darting quickly between aisles, he tried to convince his customers that every item on their lists could be found in his store.

The booths near the ice cream counter faced an aisle with a haphazard arrangement of Watkins Laxatives, tweezers, and greeting cards. While Zela and I ate our ice cream, we giggled about the NYAL Alkaline Digestive Tablets for sour stomachs and belching. While we discussed our pending adulthood, we never anticipated that our bodies would sprout stray hairs or foot corns.

As ten-year-olds, we disregarded the pastor's call to confess to God and confessed to one another instead. We leaned across a table sticky from dribbles of milkshakes and malts that Boyd neglected to wipe up between customers. We lowered our voices but felt safer amidst distracted shoppers than at home, where whispering drew our mothers' attention faster than shouting.

I gauged my sins based on my degree of regret and understood that my most unpardonable sins were those I should regret but could not. Only Zela knew that at my brother's funeral when my father rested his hand on my shoulder, I was glad my brother, Samuel, couldn't take my place. I looked to Zela for pardon. When she simply said, "That's how Daddy is with Morris," I knew she understood.

My mother waited at the dry goods store until we returned. We always found her where we left her: at the back of the store, swathing herself in fabric. Black-and-white checked silk shantung, red printed chiffon, lavender embroidered silk organza. Zela watched with envy. I watched with embarrassment. When my mother noticed us, she wordlessly tore her list into three, and we quickly gathered flour or light bulbs or any of the other staples we bought in town. My father assumed that this weekly trip required two hours of my mother's Saturday afternoon. It was the only secret we ever shared.

After *The Mansfield Journal* ran the story about the fire, Boyd Palmer was one of the first to call. He owned his father's store now, but his call reminded me of Saturday afternoons when he still scooped ice cream. It reminded me what I'd lost with Zela's death.

The awkwardness of our friendship felt temporary. One afternoon we would remember how to tell secrets again. Then I would ask her if she loved Nathaniel, if he loved her, if she regretted leaving the valley. The time never felt right and the questions felt too personal for the adult version of our friendship, so I had waited.

Condolence calls continued throughout the morning. The conversations were purposeful and hushed. I welcomed the calls. Expressing my thanks to neighbors came easier than talking to Mattie.

She wanted facts. Where. How. When. What now. I protected her from the pain these answers could create. But she looked at me like an annoying uncle too removed from childhood to realize his severed thumb trick no longer fooled anyone. I preferred her anger to her sorrow. Anger cauterized wounds.

As we prepared the midday meal, we said little. Even in the winter, I ate my largest meal at noon. The food that day lacked flavor. As I cooked, Mattie's declarations of "yuck" eliminated the onions, the boiled spinach, and the beets.

Mattie bowed her head when I set her plate in front of her. "Bless this food," I said, more for Mattie than to God. Mattie kept her head bowed as I walked between the counter and the table, carrying a plate of bread and jam.

"Amen," she said with the instruction of a Sunday school teacher.

Before I heard the first knock on the door, Mattie scooted her chair back with force. I realized she'd been listening for the slight click of the screen door. She opened the door before the second knock, only to find Retha Hilliard with one hand raised to knock and the other protectively resting on the seven-month bump of their fourth child, who had surprised them in their forties.

I often imagined what the other women in the valley would have done if they had not married. I looked for fellow farmers among them by studying their gardens. Only Eileen Russell would have been true competition; the sweet corn in her garden often produced two good ears on a stalk. Retha Hilliard was no farmer. She over-watered or under-watered her kitchen garden depending on her error the previous year. Retha would have been an investigative reporter who knitted during interviews as a purposeful distraction. I suspected she'd come to find out what I knew about the fire.

She knelt to Mattie's level, balancing herself by holding the edge of the counter, never taking her other hand from her abdomen, and said, "Oh honey, I'm so sorry." Mattie cried her first tears wrapped in Retha's hug. And for this I was grateful.

"And you," she said, motioning for me to join them on the floor. Mattie looked at me expectantly, as if we both needed a hug from Retha. I walked over and patted Mattie's shoulder. My tears would only frighten her. I offered a hand to Retha to help her to her feet.

"How's the old boy holding up?" I asked of her father-in-law. Out of my fondness for him, I tolerated Retha. George Hilliard was the only man in the valley who had not offered to buy the farm after my father died.

Instead he answered my questions while treating me as cantankerously as he did the other farmers at the grain mill, asking me the question he was known for: "When are you going to start farming those fields of yours?" I was the only one who ever answered, "As soon as you help me."

He may not have spent the time with me if he hadn't taken so much pleasure in proving his neighbors wrong. He told them after my father died that a woman could make a farm prosper as well as a man and then he taught me how. He never let on to the other men in the valley that he had helped me, and to this day if I saw him in town he'd ask me if I was still trying to get corn out of my sorry excuse for fields.

"You know George. He's happy." Retha paused, "Happy making my life miserable. If only he could help me with a ewe that dropped her water over an hour ago," she said, revealing her real reason for visiting. Retha asked for help so she could offer help. She knew me well enough to know I wouldn't accept it any other way. Then, quieter, she said, "We didn't know if family came for Zela's girl yet. I'll bring over some meals."

"I can cook, Retha," I said. "Leave me some distractions."

"I'll stop by tomorrow with clothes for her."

"Family should come for her by then. Your lamb's in danger if that ewe dropped her water over an hour ago. Where are your boys?"

Mattie had watched us with interest when we spoke of her family, but at the mention of Retha's boys, she sighed and sat back down at the table.

"They're at the implement store in Galion to price out something or other." She giggled and gave a playful smile. "You know those boys. Always busy." Retha was coy as a mother of sons, flirting on their behalf.

I did know those boys. They probably left as soon as they saw the ewe separate herself from the other ewes that Retha raised to compete at the state fair. A competition Retha never won, even with the extra expense of feeding ewes in winter to birth larger lambs.

"You know you shouldn't help deliver this lamb," I said.

"That's just a superstition. I wouldn't have come except this one's mean and she kicks."

"Do you feed her silage?"

"Does it matter?" Retha tensed. I saw in her eyes that she had miscarried other babies.

Instead of hurting her with the truth, I asked, "Do you have Ivory soap?" I stepped into my boots and shrugged on my coat. "I like it better than those fancy lubricants from the vet."

Retha had not taken a step toward her coat or the door. I held up her coat. "Well, come on. Am I going to have to dress you, too?"

Retha motioned toward Mattie, and before I could grasp that I'd forgotten her, the phone rang.

"Do you mind watching her?" I asked.

Mattie hopped from the chair and moved toward the phone as if the call could be for her.

"Let it ring," I said.

Mattie answered the phone and handed it to me. The man on the line identified himself as Zela's lawyer. He wanted to arrange a time for the reading of her will. He spoke hesitantly as if he had a habit of apologizing often.

"I don't mean to be rude," I said as I tied the laces of my boots, "but you should read the newspaper. The fire destroyed everything. If she left me anything, give it to her girl. I've got to go."

"I'm sorry, so sorry, but we must take care of this immediately."

"If I don't leave right now, my neighbor may lose her lamb and ewe."

"You must be at the reading of the will."

"Mail me a letter. I assure you no one else wants me there."

Mattie asked Retha if I was talking to someone about her mom and dad. Retha shushed her and leaned toward me.

"You need to be present," he said, "because you are her daughter's guardian."

I slowly stood from tying my boots and leaned against the counter. "I'm not family. That can't be."

Retha moved closer to me. She would spread this confusion through town before I sorted out the lawyer's error.

"I must go or you'll owe my neighbor a lamb. Call me tonight." I hung up on him and zipped my coat.

"Will you watch her?" I asked Retha, as if we had not been interrupted.

Nearly the entire valley separated my farm from the Hilliard farm. Their fields marked the end of the land once owned by the Brubakers. Many considered their fencerow, garlanded with goldenrod and wild phlox in the summer and clusters of wild grapes in the fall, as the signpost for leaving the valley. Their house and barn jutted out onto a bend in the road, making the four hundred acres that spread behind them seem even more expansive. They had the only white barn in the valley, which was a sign of prosperity from a time when a lead-based whitewash cost fourteen cents a pound and red cost eight.

This gambrel-roofed barn, constructed from walnut wood on a fieldstone base, was the reason Mr. Hilliard chose this farm. They said when his father-in-law, a Brubaker, offered him the choice between two farms, Mr. Hilliard said he'd make the fields worthy of a barn that beautiful. Mr. Hilliard called the story sentimental, but he never denied it.

I found him in the back of the barn sitting in a lawn chair with his cane across his lap, apparently to prod the ewe away from him. His cheeks had wrinkled into hollow pockets like a pepper left too long on the vine. His oxygen tube strung from his nose to the oxygen tank hidden behind two bales of straw. He told me that after he died I should mount the tank as a scarecrow in my blueberry patch.

"What took you so long?" He jabbed his cane in the direction of the pregnant ewe that leaned against the side of the pen and ground her teeth.

"Don't you keep up with the news?"

"Haven't seen good use for a newspaper since we got plumbing."

The four-by-four birthing pen smelled like lye and fresh straw. Retha had prepared for the birth. A slight warmth hovered around the five ewes, shorn to share their body heat with the lambs.

"Why would you get a newspaper when you have Retha?"

He chuckled. "Where is that girl?"

"She's watching the Brubaker girl at my place." He would never recognize the name Morgan. In this valley, Zela and Mattie would always be Brubakers.

The ewe walked in a small circle and nested by pawing at the straw. "Are you here to help me or distract me?" I asked.

"Never knew you to be distractible, darling." Banter I once feared as flirtatious had become comfortably familiar long ago. Then he asked, "What do you need?"

"I need your longest gloves and Ivory soap for now. Don't get too settled. You'll need to help."

He pointed with his cane to the oxygen tank, a doctor's recommendation enforced by Retha. Mr. Hilliard had told me if his family was going to muzzle him, they might as well shoot him.

"Are you going to let that slow you down?"

The ewe dug at a different spot in the straw before she grunted and strained with a push. As I swabbed her with disinfectant, she didn't resist me. She had accepted the pain as a permanent condition.

"I thought this one was a kicker," I said as Mr. Hilliard tottered toward the supply shelf.

Clearly he had not heard me as he raised his cane above him to nudge the wooden shelf held by a few nails in pegboard. The Ivory soap hopped along the shelf as he jostled it. After a few ineffectual prods, he swept his cane across the shelf above him, knocking a bottle of iodine, towels, and the soap to the floor. Disregarding the noise, I busied myself with the spigot to fill a bucket with water.

Mr. Hilliard tucked the Ivory soap under his armpit and slung the green rubber gloves over his shoulder. Then he wheeled his oxygen tank with one hand and supported himself on his cane with the other. The ewe toddled around me, preoccupied by her determination to nest. She needed to push.

I worried that we had already lost the lamb. I would have completed the examination by now if I'd left Mr. Hilliard sitting on the chair, but he needed more struggle than his family allowed him.

I coated my gloved hands in diluted soap and said, "I can't do this without you."

"Keep lying to me, girl. I like it," he said. "You take it from here."

"No doing. Get over here and hold her legs."

"I'll get all tangled up." He wiggled the tube to his oxygen.

"Take it off."

"You're trying to do me in," he said harshly, but he unhooked the tube from his nostrils and waited a moment as if anticipating death. As he helped me roll the ewe onto her side, he said, "You're going to lose this lamb."

I adjusted the shoulder-length gloves and then slowly eased my hand into the warm birth canal. The canal contracted, gripping my forearm like a blood pressure cuff.

Grasping a hard knob, hoof or nose, I stroked my hand along it, determining it was a leg. I held it between two fingers and rubbed my other hand up the legs, searching for the nose, hoping it was merely a tight birth.

"Breech?" he asked.

"Nope. I've got her front hooves. She can't decide if she wants to come or stay. Hand me some twine."

With the heel of my hand, I guided the twined legs into the ewe's body and nestled the lamb's head between its legs. I knelt to gain leverage while not losing my grip above the lamb's knees. My arm cramped as I worked with the contractions and slowly guided the hoofs and head through the birth canal.

"Retha can't do this once she has a young one," he said.

"They don't stay babies forever. She could teach those other children of hers about lambing for a season."

I'd ignored a nagging feeling that I had forgotten something. Had I shut off the space heater in my office? The stove in the kitchen? Did I have the money for my uncle? As I tugged the mucus-covered lamb onto straw that smelled like October, I remembered that Zela was dead. My breath caught in my chest.

The lamb, covered in phlegm, seemed too stunned to breathe. Usually this pitiful sight drew the ewe to vigorously lick the lamb to life. But she stumbled toward Mr. Hilliard. I wiped the lamb's nose and tickled it with a piece of straw to encourage its first breath.

"The ewe's a first-timer. For all she knows she's not constipated anymore," Mr. Hilliard said as I hoisted the lamb by her back ankles. I swung the lamb in small circles to force the diaphragm up and down. The lamb sneezed to life. I laid her near the ewe so she would lick her.

"You'd think she'd have some instinct," I said when the ewe walked away from the lamb. She responded as if we were grafting an orphan lamb to a lactating ewe.

"Life's more about choices than instinct."

"You can encourage instinct with Vapor Rub," I said, though Retha would bottle-feed before she took the trouble every morning to smear Vapor Rub on the ewe's nose and the same on the lamb's anus for when the ewe sniffed the lamb for a trace of her milk.

Mr. Hilliard had hidden his difficulty breathing until he hooked the tube back in his nose. His tank scratched through the straw as he dragged the lamb by the scruff of its neck toward the ewe. He buried the ewe's face in the lamb until she licked.

Chapter Three

An abandoned field in the valley would have a five o'clock shadow of pines and ash within a few years. Within ten years, the forest would reclaim it as its own. This was not the flat land of Ohio; it was soil of clay, limestone, gypsum, and shale. Some farmers dug holes to bury their rocks while others hauled them to woods they never intended to farm. The valley did not offer up its spring-fed soil easily. My Uncle Charlie was merely another obstacle to remove before I could call this land mine.

When Uncle Charlie arrived the day after the fire, he paid no heed to Mattie, who had slept all morning under two Afghans in the living room. I had lit the fire for her and failed to interest her in musty children's books I found in the attic.

Even if Charlie read in the newspaper about the fire, today was the first of February, and I had expected him.

He mopped his nose with a handkerchief and then stuffed it into his suit pocket. The wind had shifted his hairpiece slightly to the left. It had taken years for Charlie to create himself, and he did not see retirement as a call to change anything. He still wore his banking suits as if he drove from his office to the farm to collect his money. A silver chain looped pretentiously into his breast pocket, which hid my grandfather's pocket watch, a Waltham Riverside that kept perfect time. Pride was the first and greatest sin, according to my father, yet he had flirted with damnation every Sunday when he shined the Waltham and ceremoniously clicked open the silver-chrome case to time the preacher's sermons. I sold the watch to Charlie the year grain prices dropped.

The room held Charlie's attention as if he watched a picture show. "Knocked out your father's front teeth in that doorway."

My father told me a mule kicked out his originals, but I said, "He told me."

Charlie laughed an old man's laugh that sputtered like water from an unused spigot. "Best punch I ever threw."

I did not know of this particular fight, yet I had sensed every one of their fights when my father tensed up at the sound of Charlie's car on our lane. When my uncle walked beside him, my father lost any confidence he found in working his fields. My hatred of my uncle felt as old as my father's fear of him.

"When will you tire of driving out here and give me the land?"

"You're not as close to ending these payments as you act. You never show a bit of respect, Dottie Connell."

I took my record book from the top of the refrigerator and flipped it open. "Eight years and three months." Every third month Charlie wrote out a receipt that I stapled in the book. In the back of the book I kept a copy of the loan agreement. I kept the original in a safe in my office. My father had never asked for receipts. When Charlie told my father the amount of the payments, my father always paid. "If your conscience ever allows, you'll find those lost records. You and I both know my father paid this debt long ago," I said.

"You've only started paying your father's debt."

"Whatever he did to you can't be much worse than making his child pay for him."

"You should have let him leave this land when he wanted to."

I counted the bills in the envelope labeled "My Land" and handed him a fistful of bills. "Don't waste any more of my time."

Family remained family to my father and mother, who spread a full Sunday dinner for Charlie, Aunt Georgia, and their children on the Sundays he collected. My father handed the money to Charlie in a handshake, so he could, presumably, pretend his brother visited for reasons other than cash. I kept Charlie's payment envelope on top of the refrigerator and never invited him in. In the fourteen years since my father's death, Charlie had learned this routine and rarely removed his coat. As he clasped the money with a silver monogrammed clip, he said, "Your cousin will be in town soon. Maybe by the time I bring him along, you'll remember how to treat family."

"A man should start to wonder when all three of his children scatter across the country." I handed him his hat and opened the door. "I don't have time for visiting. Don't bother to bring him by."

I would not play hostess like my mother, who ordered hotel restaurant cookbooks for recipes to impress my Aunt Georgia. My mother had not dressed up the family on Sundays for God, but in case Aunt Georgia visited with Uncle Charlie after church.

"He wants to see the family farm," Charlie said, before he secured his hat and tucked his cane over his arm.

"Calling us family won't make it so," I said. I leaned past him and swung open the screen door. The door slammed behind him when he left. As always, my last words hung as stiffly and awkwardly as underwear on the clothesline with company on the porch. I would never have the last word as long as Charlie held the deed to this farm.

Chapter Four

The morning of Zela's funeral I filled a thermos half with coffee and the other half with cream so I could share the hot drink with Mattie, who had slept fitfully the past two nights. The walls of my eighty-year-old house provided partitions, not privacy. Over the years, the walls served to separate the brothers from the sisters and the children from the parents, but late at night, the house had no walls. It unsettled me to wake suddenly in this darkness and hear the ticking of the cuckoo clock under my bed and the shuddering refrigerator as if it sat in the corner of my room. The noises felt as pervasive as God, whose existence frightened me during dark hours, when there were no distractions to quiet Him.

Mattie crawled from her bed every night. She swaddled herself in quilts next to the radiator as if she were a poult who would give up food and water for the warmth of a heat lamp. Last night she called for her mother and cried when I came to her. I listened to her crying from the kitchen as I heated up milk in a saucepan and flavored it with a dash of vanilla. As she sipped the milk, I sat on the ladder-back desk chair near her nest and resolved that she would not go another night without sleep.

We would not attend the funeral. We would work. Grief was a spoiled child. Coddling it only made it cry for attention. Sleep earned by a day's work would serve her better than relatives expecting her to cry. I had buried my family. Fewer attended each funeral, but after my brother's death, the numbers could only be expected to decrease. His service drew every valley mother who feared the possibility of losing a child, and every father who understood my own father's despair at losing his only son.

My father told us not to fuss with a funeral home and to bury him in a pine box. So my mother prepared his body for the viewing in our sitting room. She cut the back of a suit jacket that he outgrew long ago and dressed him as she first saw him, when he visited Erie to do business on his father's behalf. She bought a silk tie from Montgomery Ward and slicked back his hair with Harmony Quintine Hair Tonic. After she left the room, I slipped off his Sunday shoes and socks, wishing I had time before others arrived to lace on his work boots to cover his feet, which were as white and wrinkled as my mother's hands. I preferred thinking of him barefoot rather than stuffed into the shoes he always took off during the drive to and from church.

My mother's death came weeks after my father's. She followed him only twice in her life, first from Erie to the farm and then into death. My mother's funeral was the only one planned. In her precise Palmer penmanship she had written out the order of service, which was to include the hymn "I'm Going Home." She had sewn her dress, which was a green more vibrant than any natural growing thing, and clipped a pair of fake pearl earrings to the neckline so I could find them. I gave the dress and instructions to Wiseman's Funeral Home, where she had pre-ordered a casket that demonstrated an extravagance that only surfaced during her life in occasional deliveries of expensive lace and magazine subscriptions. She made the payments for ten years. Wilbur Wiseman, who had recently assumed his father's position as the funeral director, attempted to comfort mourners by doling out tissues. I flustered him when I asked if I could return the casket for the least expensive one and cash out the difference. He handed me a tissue and then said yes. My crops had not produced enough to make the payment I owed my uncle.

Grieving could not come in the office of a funeral director or even at a funeral. Grief was like stepping on rocks in May. One could only toughen to the pain by walking over it, not by standing politely at a funeral, dabbing away tears.

I saw little point in driving to Zela's funeral in Mansfield. I would find work we could do in the heated machine shed, because I doubted that Zela had packed warm work clothes for Mattie. The drapes were drawn in the spare room, and the resulting darkness shrouded the hallway at the top of the stairs in shadow. I drew back the cotton curtains, stiff and oily with dust. Dust motes swayed as slow as algae in the pond. Mattie slept in the bed, clutching the blankets close to her chin. She had not migrated to the radiator after I packed her under the covers at three in the morning.

I squeezed her shoulder. "It's time to get up."

"It's too cold." She slid farther under the pile of blankets until I coaxed her by tapping the lump. Slowly crawling from the bed, she leaned into me with an abandon I never shared with my mother. I combed her dark hair with my fingers. It was practical affection because any other felt awkward.

"Sleep," she said.

"We have work to do," I said, stricter than I intended. I wanted her to lose this day amongst others of waking early for work.

I made the bed so Mattie would not retreat to it. She still wore the rumpled tan corduroy jumper with a green turtleneck and matching ribbed stockings that she'd worn for almost three days. I had not realized until she drank her milk last night that I should have prompted her to change into a nightgown.

"Do you have any other clothes with you?"

"I don't know."

I opened the closet, which was crowded with storage boxes, and then looked under the bed and found that Zela had left a red leather suitcase. The silver buckles had not been unfastened enough to wrinkle the leather straps. The leather was unscuffed, awaiting travel. Like everything Zela had owned, the suitcase had a department-store sheen. Her life could have been photographed for a magazine.

I opened the suitcase, which was too large for an overnight bag, hoping Zela had thought to pack pants rather than a skirt. A small grief clenched my jaw at the sight of corduroy pants and a heavy, gray wool sweater. Under the outfit, she had packed a pair of long underwear still clipped with the price tag. Why hadn't she told me she wanted Mattie to milk the cows with me? I lifted the long underwear, looking for socks. For a moment, I chuckled at the number of pants, turtlenecks, and sweaters that Zela had rolled like bandages. She had always responded to uncertainty by over-preparing. She had taken wool stockings on her honeymoon to Florida because she read that the temperature dropped at night, and she had kept an emergency kit in her car that included a toothbrush.

Mattie sat on the bed while I stacked the clothes beside me, searching for socks. Under the pants, I found a layer of dresses, rolled as neatly as the layer of pants. A few price tags dangled from dresses that were too lightweight for Mattie to wear until spring. I dug through the clothes, shoving aside shirts, jumpers, and pajamas. I tried to hide my concern from Mattie, who crawled down from the bed to pick out her clothes.

"We bought our suitcases at Reed's," Mattie said, as she took off her socks and dug through the suitcase to find a clean pair.

"Looks like your mom wanted you to stay with me for a bit," I admitted to her for the first time. I wondered if Mattie's apparent relief came from her mother wanting her to stay with me or that I said *a bit* rather than forever.

I should have noticed that Mattie had brought a suitcase rather than an overnight bag. I should have called Zela and asked why Mattie needed so many clothes to spend the night. It disturbed me more to realize that Zela may have wanted me to call.

Mattie and I would spend the morning of Zela's funeral in the machine shed. I flicked on the overhead heaters and hung my jacket on the peg under two rows of ball caps. My winters were spent in this shed, overhauling machines more temperamental than the horses that once pulled my father's plows.

The shed smelled like work. The machines sweated gasoline and oil, and clumps of earth still clung to the tires. The year I bought my Massey 300 with a three-row header, I built the thirty-six by seventy-six foot machine shed. In the unheated section, I parked the Massey, the mower, and the tractors. In the heated section, the ceiling rose high enough that I could hook a tractor to chains and hoist it for repair, and the sub-floor allowed me to work on machines too heavy to lift. I closed the door separating the machines from the shop so it would heat faster. Mattie thrust her hands into her coat pockets.

"If you leave your coat on in here, it won't keep you warm when you leave," I said, as I rearranged the clutter on my desk, looking for two coffee mugs. My mugs and ball caps advertised seed, machinery, and anything else from the "Ag" and State fairs, where I'd collected them from representatives' tables over the years. I ripped a paper towel off the holder over the workbench and swiped out the dust in the bottom of my mug. Mattie cringed.

"It's not as dirty in here as you think." I poured her coffee into the thermos lid. She reluctantly removed her coat before accepting it from me.

"I shouldn't drink coffee," she told me, swiftly gaining authority by placing restrictions on herself.

"The coffee only flavors the milk."

"Is the milk from your cow?"

"That's where milk comes from."

She sniffed the coffee and then slowly poured it onto the floor. The muddy river of coffee curled through the dirt floor of the shed. I handed her a rag even though the floor already had birthmarks of brake fluid and oil. She pressed lightly on the cloth, dabbing at the dirt as though she'd spilled grape juice on white carpet. Zela had trained her well.

"You're a better worker than most if you don't want a coffee break. Let's get to work," I said.

I opened the incinerator door and positioned boxes of trash close enough to the door so that Mattie could easily scoop in the advertisement circulars, week-old newspapers, and scraps of paper. I tossed in a few handfuls before looking at Mattie expectantly. She came closer to the box.

"Don't you have a trash man?"

I thrust in two more handfuls of papers. "You can't be afraid to work around here." I pointed to the three boxes. "Those are yours to empty."

As I walked to my desk, I glanced at Mattie, who flung an envelope into the incinerator. "You can hold more than that," I said. Work only soothed by moving too fast to think of anything but the task at hand.

When I built the shed six years earlier, I lined the building with pegboard as high as my reach. Over the years I covered the walls with every size belt, jumper cable, chain, hose, shovel, and rake. My best intentions to organize were strewn throughout the shed. There were plastic trays for washers and bolts, and hooks for stations around the saw and the welder. When I welded,

I wasted five minutes looking for the mask I'd hung in a hurry on any open peg.

I decided to clear my desk first. On top of the clutter was graph paper with sketches of the fields and my plans for planting that I'd started the day Zela brought Mattie. I had meant to rethink the order of the row crops down the side hill but had not thought of the fields in three days.

My mind went over the last time I saw Zela like a debit and credit sheet I could not balance. But I could not continue to wait for her return, neglecting my work in favor of inventing work for Mattie. I had endured her presence. I had not yet considered adapting to it.

My hired hand, Stanley, hung his coat on a peg by the door and filled a cup with coffee from my thermos. Men did not remain long on my farm. Most hired hands could only tolerate working for a woman one season. I hired Stanley because he lied to me and then confessed his lie, and confessing a lie required more integrity than not telling one at all.

Stanley's foreignness was apparent even before his tongue revealed the habit of another language. His sandy hair, which fanned flat over his forehead, was longer than the close-cropped cuts of local boys. He had only asked for a room and two meals in exchange for outdoor work.

His fixed stare on his boots had revealed that he'd grown accustomed to refusal. When I had asked which farms in the valley he'd been to, he named them all. Then he admitted the truth. He was German, not Belgian as he had first claimed. Origins still mattered in the valley, especially if the valley was not one's origin. Plenty from the valley traced their ancestors to Germany, but their families had come to this valley long before either war, and they still remembered the names of the boys who had not come home from Europe or the Pacific.

Stanley was one of the few hired men who appeared grateful rather than resigned when I offered work. Since Mattie's arrival, my days had lost their rhythm, and I hadn't considered how Stanley spent his time.

"Little one, you go play," he said as he picked up the box and dumped it into the incinerator. In one movement, he eliminated two hours of work I'd dreamed up to occupy Mattie.

"That's Mattie's job," I said. If I'd hired a man to replace him, he could not have looked more stunned. He lowered the box and studied the child before looking at me.

"If I need to burn trash, then ask. Do not put a child to work to tell me."

He heaved the other two boxes into the incinerator, lit it, and clamped the door shut. When he first arrived on the farm, he would drop a task to rush in to finish mine, seemingly conditioned to finish a woman's work before he completed his own. This was the only time I threatened to fire him.

"I asked you to change the plugs on the tractor. Have you?"

Mattie paid little attention to us. She gathered empty boxes and crumpled rags strewn around the workbenches. I hadn't realized she had paid any heed when I told her we needed to clean the shed. Stanley came closer to me and motioned toward Mattie as if to explain why. He had chopped wood that morning. The chill of snow still lingered on him and flecks of ash were caught in his hair.

His breath was warm and smelled like the caramels that he scooped from my desk drawer. I worried again that I should fix larger meals for him. I had never cooked for a man.

"She might get hurt," he said quietly.

"Last I checked, your only job today is to get the tractor running."

He hesitated, as he often did, and I wondered what conversations we would have if he did not fear me. He nodded. "I understand. I'm sorry I took your job, little one," he said.

"I'm Mattie."

"Good to meet you," he said. He knelt in front of her and offered her his hand.

He returned to the tractor, and I set Mattie to sorting nails, washers, and wrenches scattered across my worktable. To find a washer I typically brushed my hand over the table as my mother had spread flour over the counter before she rolled dough. As Mattie compared a cotter pin to a tooth washer, she pursed her mouth with all the concentration of her grandmother Brubaker, who lifted scalding canning jars with pudgy fingers burnt from years of thrusting her hands into steaming dishwater.

Mattie's upturned nose and dark eyes with black lashes reminded me why so many mothers in the valley had wanted Zela for their sons. She appeared to have enough spunk to birth a family and enough docility to submit to a man. Zela had surprised everyone when she drove a half-hour each way to Mansfield to work as a medical transcriptionist after high school. She said nothing, even to me, about the deliberateness of it all. Zela secured an engagement to a doctor before he was drafted.

My desk was cluttered with a box of WD-40, blue shop towels, used and unused, and screwdrivers. I cleared a shelf in the back of the barn for the box of WD-40 and then gathered up bottles of brake fluid, hydraulic jack oil, and steering fluid and lined them on the shelf. From the bin of cans that I would crush and bury when the ground thawed, I found two Maxwell House cans and filled them with various sizes of screwdrivers.

Mattie hopped down from her stool at the bench before I realized she'd gone. She returned a few minutes later with Stanley following her, wiping his hands on a blue shop rag and tucking it in his back pocket. He sat on the stool in front of the tool bench.

"These two are easy." He picked up a flat washer and a split washer. "Put the ones that look broken in this bin and the whole circle in the other."

Outside the shed, Banjo barked, paused, and barked again. If he merely spotted a chipmunk in his patrol, he would bark in rapid succession. Company concerned him less than a rodent. He greeted any car driving down the lane with a lazier, slower bark. I brushed aside cobwebs, lacy with dust, from the window above my desk and licked my thumb to shine a small peephole in the dirt. Banjo ran toward a car, which drove too cautiously down the middle of the lane to be local.

"You two keep working. I'll get us dinner." I glanced at my watch. It was almost one o'clock and neither Mattie nor Stanley had complained of hunger, though Mattie sucked loudly on a caramel. I opened the top drawer where I kept the Brach's caramels to wash down my throat when sawdust tickled it. Stanley had taken another handful to share.

Banjo ran to me as I left the shed. Snow bearded his red Airedale curls. He trotted beside me as I came to the hill leading to the house. A man in a dark black suit and a heavy wool coat surveyed the farm. He had the stature of a Brubaker, too tall for dairy farming and arms too thick with strength to wear a suit jacket with ease. Brubakers were built to clear land and haul crops into barns and silos. There had been a time when a Brubaker would have walked into our house and sat at the kitchen table so as not to rush us.

As I neared the house, I knew this Brubaker was Morris. I had not talked to him in seventeen years, but I knew him from the way he swiped a match on the bottom of his shoe and lit his cigarette. The smoke blew as wildly as his thinning blond hair. Even though he wore a suit, I had difficulty thinking of him as a lawyer.

No one first meeting Morris would describe him as handsome, but not a girl in the valley would have turned down a proposal from Morris Brubaker. He had the walk of a man who knew himself. His dark eyes distracted anyone from noticing that they were set too close to his thin nose. He had a wide jaw that suggested the Brubakers' Germanic origins. He was the rare sort of man who was liked by men and women and not disliked by either for his influence over both.

I fought an impulse to call out to him as though he still waited for me with anticipation. As I neared the porch, he turned toward me. He squinted against the cold or scowled; I could no longer read him. I took the steps to the porch slowly, wanting him to offer the first greeting. He walked toward the door, and I opened it without saying hello.

Morris hung his coat on the hook by the door, as he used to do after a day of working with my father. He ate more dinners at our house than at his own after my brother died. My mother spent her egg money in extravagant grief to see a boy, who was the age my brother should have been, working the farm. My father complained that the Brubakers should pay him for making a farmer out of their son; I only wished he had succeeded. These were conversations I wanted to have with Morris. I stomped the snow from my boots and kicked them off next to the door.

"Morris," I finally said by way of a greeting. He nodded, and I remembered this silence as his anger. I poured the remainder of the morning coffee into a saucepan and turned the burner to medium.

"Where's Mattie?" he finally asked.

"Machine shed, sorting nails." My hand brushed my shoulder, a nervous habit I had not lost after cropping my hair close to my head. My hair felt too short and my neck too exposed. I forced a laugh. "She's a Brubaker."

"Why didn't you bring her?"

I wanted to reach out and take his hands to make him look me in the eyes. Who else knew Zela as we had? I wanted to hold him and be held by him as we admitted that Zela was gone. But I sat across from him and hid my rough hands under my thighs that spread the width of the chair.

"Mattie deserved better," I said.

The coffee bubbled gently on the stove and I stood to pour it. I lingered near the stove longer than needed, wanting it to be the cause of the uncertain warmth that spread through my stomach. I could not settle on a single emotion. Morris stirred in me two decades of feelings: hatred, comfort, and desire.

I poured warmed coffee into mugs. "Do you still take cream?"

"Did I ever take cream?" He ran his fingers through his hair, only stirring up the static. "Everyone was there, Dottie. We even drove my mother over from the home. Everyone asked why a child was not at her parents' funeral."

I set his coffee in front of him. It looked lonesome and inhospitable. "I have zucchini bread in the freezer. Would you like a slice with your coffee?"

"What couldn't have waited until tomorrow?" He looked behind me. "Is there more coffee? I don't take cream."

"I can reheat some more."

He waved away the request. "Reboiled coffee will be better with cream." He sipped the coffee.

"Your hired man can milk the cows. Any neighbor in this valley could run the farm for a day."

"It didn't do us one bit of good to go to Samuel's funeral."

"It made it real." Morris grasped the coffee mug with both hands and looked around the kitchen. As I followed his gaze, I saw how little had changed. The red polka dot curtains with the red ribbon trim were faded to the color of the rusty underbelly of a tractor. The colander and pans dangled on the same hooks over the stove. A new calendar hung from an old nail near the telephone.

"You missed Zela's funeral," he said.

I glanced out the window for Mattie, a habit as new as scratching poison ivy. "I stayed home for Mattie, not for myself."

"Zela would have wanted her there."

"She would have wanted what was best for Mattie," I said. "You can never grieve with others as well as you can grieve on your own."

"And you called yourself her friend."

"You act like I drove to Mansfield and set fire to her house."

He tipped his mug back and forth as if he could read the future in the coffee grounds that floated to the surface. "It would be worse if I accused you of what I really think happened."

"I can't think of what would be worse."

"It's like everything else. You were too focused on yourself to notice that she needed you. You must have ignored some suspicion."

I looked out the window toward the machine shed. Mattie trudged through the snow with her coat splayed open by the wind. She shied away from Banjo, who followed her to the house.

"What could I have been suspicious about? Should I have asked her if she checked the wiring in her attic? Or should I have asked her if Nathaniel smoked in bed?" I voiced the two theories put forth in the newspaper.

"You know as well as I do that it wasn't coincidence that Mattie wasn't in the house."

Morris struck a match on the corner of the kitchen table and lit another cigarette. He stared out the window taking short, nervous puffs. I wanted to reach for the pack and light a cigarette to occupy my hands, though I had only ever smoked with Morris.

Morris tapped the ashes into his half-drunk coffee. "Just tell me why you didn't call anyone when Zela left her here."

Mattie yelled hello to her uncle before she fully opened the door. She ran into the kitchen smiling and crawled onto his lap. Cold had burned her fingers bright red. Morris rubbed her hands between his and held onto her as if she had plunged into the lake without knowing how to swim.

"Don't leave yet," she said, as she climbed from his lap and ran toward the stairs. Morris stubbed out the cigarette on the saucer and glanced toward the ceiling. Mattie was opening and shutting the bureau drawers in the spare room.

"The police chief found gasoline cans." Morris paused and watched for my reaction. "Four five-gallon cans. The bedroom was drenched in it. The fire wouldn't have taken off like it did without it."

"She dowsed the bedroom," I said, trying to hold together the image of Zela looking out at her family's old farm from the sitting room and shaking a five-gallon gas can when she returned home.

"Four cans, Dottie," he said, as if I should find meaning in his emphasis. "More than someone keeps in his garage for a lawn mower."

"From my shed?" I asked, not because I believed this, but because I heard his accusation in his tone.

Morris nodded and then asked, "Why didn't you tell anyone she changed the will?"

I had given little thought to the lawyer's phone call telling me Zela had left Mattie to me. This error was not something to correct until after the funeral. Yet Morris's accusations stopped me from mentioning this. Instead I said, "I didn't ask to raise Mattie."

"Was it for the money?"

"I haven't heard word one about money or gasoline cans, not even in the papers."

"The Mansfield police chief is Nathaniel's cousin. He told me this wouldn't get out. And don't act like you wouldn't use the inheritance to get this farm in your name."

"You might as well call me Uncle Charlie." The chair squealed as I shoved back from the table. I slammed the pan into the sink and cranked on the hot water. "You have insulted me enough for one afternoon. Get out of my house."

He moved close enough to me that I lost the distractions of his suit and the diamonds in his wedding band. I had to look him in the eye. He softened his tone. "You and I both know you'd give up everything to own this farm."

"I will own this farm in eight years. I've nearly paid the debt without you and wouldn't settle for an easy way out now." I lowered my voice, though the floor upstairs creaked as Mattie walked down the hall. "I can assure you of one thing. I would never have taken on a child who will only slow me down."

Morris shook his head. "You have fought so viciously for such a small piece of this earth."

I knew from the methodic thump on the stairs that Mattie was dragging her suitcase behind her. "You should leave," I said, wanting him out of the house before he saw her with her suitcase.

"I'm ready to go home now," Mattie announced as she came into the kitchen.

"Does she know?" Morris asked quietly.

"Mattie, your uncle is leaving." I handed him his coat. He took it and did not put it on until he reached his car.

That night I stood by Mattie's door and listened to her steady breaths. She had not slept this well since Zela left her with me. Finally, she slept without crying. No matter what Morris said, I had done right by her.

Chapter Five

"Stanley," I called quietly into the darkness of the machine shed. The floodlight buzzing outside emitted a faint light too dim to cast shadows in the shed. It was only seven in the evening, but it was darker than summer nights when I slept through these blotted hours.

I had every right to turn on the lights and poke around my shed for missing gasoline cans. Yet at this hour, the shed belonged to Stanley. Six years back, I built a small room onto the back of the shed for temporary housing. Two cots, a card table, and my mother's rocking chair furnished the space. Over the years, a few men added shelves made from scrap lumber to hold their clothes and dishes. Stanley cluttered the shelves with his carvings. In the evenings, he etched animals into pine, balsam, and ash. Black bears, bobcats, wolves, cobras. They bared their teeth and stiffened in the moment before an attack.

He washed himself and his dishes with the hose in the corner nearest the drain and left his bar of soap propped on a ledge above the hose; it filled the shed with his scent. In my youth, when the mysteries of men enticed me, I would have breathed answers in that smell. But I was older now and suspicious of answers.

"Stanley," I whispered again, hoping he would not reply. I knew little of his routines in these hours. I hesitated to enter the shed too quickly, assuming he shared my practice of showering in the evening to wash away a day's work.

Soft grunts came from his room. A splinter of light outlined the door where shadows rapidly shifted at the foot of it. I stopped at the sound of a fight. Solid jabs pounded into someone too weak to fight back. With my hand outstretched, I walked in the dark toward the room. Farming had buffed away any indecision from my actions; hesitating could lead to lost limbs or worse. I opened Stanley's door before deciding if I should knock or leave.

He stood with his fists raised and his feet firmly angled in a boxer's stance toward a stack of straw bales with a sheet tossed over them. He lowered his fists and wiped his brow. Before I could apologize for opening the door, he put on his shirt.

"Who's winning?" I asked.

"You don't knock?" He looked down as he buttoned his shirt.

"Not when I think someone's assaulting my hired man."

Stanley laughed and shook his head. "And you save me?" He walked over and patted me on the shoulder so

I felt every five-foot-six-inches of my body. His extra five inches had never made him look taller. He laughed, so I swung my fist with my full weight into his stomach, which resisted my punch. As I stepped back, stunned, he laughed harder.

"So you won't be calling me to save you," I said, trying to recover what I had lost in that punch.

"I call you first," he said, then he mimicked my punch in the straw bales. "You fight, then think. You make a good soldier."

"I wouldn't take orders well."

He nodded and sat on the cot. "This is true." Comfortably propped on his elbows, he never appeared this relaxed.

"This space suiting you?" I asked. More carvings lined his shelves than in the fall when I had stopped in to tell him where to find his breakfast and dinner on the porch each day. He'd driven a nail into the stud by the door to hang his brown hat, too floppy to be a local boy's. A tin mug and straight-edged razor sat on an otherwise empty shelf.

"For now," he said. He wiped sweat from his forehead, smoothing his hair to the side. The look suited him.

"You moving on?" I shoved my hands in my pockets to appear less anxious than I felt. I had too many concerns to find another hired hand by spring.

"When you ask me to."

"How about I give you a little money each month? Not much, maybe enough to save up for a better hat."

"Room and meals are enough."

"I know that. But your carving knife won't last forever, and I can't have bored workers in the evenings. You keep to yourself, and I like that."

"I'd like if you buy me a stove."

"My cooking's that bad?"

He paused, and then with a mischievous smile as if I presented a dare, he said, "You cook like you work. Fast. Your potatoes are hard and your eggs runny."

"Is that so?" I asked. "Keep talking and you'll be cooking for us."

"Outdoor work is all I asked for. You made me dream by offering a new hat."

"Let's keep it at a hat for now. If things work out, we'll talk about a stove."

I patted the bales of straw on my way out. "I've never known this straw to do anything to you. Go easy on it."

He nodded with mock seriousness, and I shut the door behind me. Turning on the lights disoriented me as I looked for familiar objects in the shed. The Lincoln arc welder was now to my left instead of shoved in the corner near the barrels of Trans-Hydraulic fluid. The bins that Mattie filled were labeled and nailed into the pegboard over the tool bench. Stanley had organized the shed. I considered thanking him but decided to let him think it motivated my offer for pay.

I propped open the door to the unheated portion of the shed with a rock kept nearby for that purpose. I expected to find the four gasoline cans missing. Since Morris had implied it, I knew Zela had taken them from the bottom shelf. They were easier to lift at that angle. I imagined gasoline-caked dust would rim where the cans had sat. Four circles of unsoiled wood would stare back at me. I came at night because all day I had envisioned the missing cans as I washed sheets and vacuumed the house. I wanted only to run my hand over the shelf to confirm it.

More than the absent cans, the missing snow sled surprised me. I kept the Flexible Flyer with the rusting runners first for the children I planned to have and then for nostalgia for my childhood. Four sets of thin tracks cut through the dirt from the shelf to the door. The forty-pound weight of the five-gallon cans had not dissuaded Zela. She had pulled one can at a time to her car and then taken the sled with her. A pressure akin to a firm handshake gripped my stomach. Her deliberateness saddened me more than her death. I sighed in resignation to her stubbornness and to the clearest vision of her since she died.

A glint of silver reflected a bit of light from the shed. Nothing typically shone in my garage that resembled an implement store after a dust storm. I leaned over two barrels of antifreeze and lifted out a red leather suitcase. I realized before I unzipped it that Zela never intended for me to wear the aprons. She had brought them for herself.

I ignored the clang of a dinner bell as I lifted sturdy pants Zela would never have worn in Mansfield. A few dresses filled only a small corner of the suitcase. I thrust my hand deep into the suitcase to see how many layers of clothing filled it. A small black box, wedged in the deep center, held Zela's wedding ring.

At the second hollow echo of the dinner bell, I remembered Mattie the morning after the fire standing on the picnic table ringing the bell, and I ran from the shed without my coat. How long had I left her? I envied mothers who had nine months to grow accustomed to the weight of a child and whose hollowed wombs created an instinct to remember their children.

I looked for Mattie but saw Retha Hilliard instead. She yelled a friendly hello and motioned for me to come inside as if I were walking up the lane to her house. She returned to the kitchen where every light shone. On snowy winter evenings, I walked by moonlight to the dark house, which had more potential for life than a house lonely with empty lit rooms. Yet this evening two women fluttered in my illumined kitchen like moths.

The Goswells' Ford was parked near the house, which could only mean that Alice Goswell had come with Retha. Had I not left Mattie alone in the house, I would have climbed into my truck and honked as I drove down my lane. When Alice offered help, you accepted it on God's behalf. Alice paid no heed to refusals for her too-tart, cherry sympathy pies. She made the pies for God's approval, not for the needy. He apparently looked for the appearance of good deeds, so He wouldn't notice if she skimped on the sugar.

I knew as I walked toward the house that I would never tell anyone about the suitcase. I would drop it into the incinerator some night and forget I had found it.

When I entered the kitchen, Retha nodded to me. She leaned the full weight of her pregnancy into scrubbing my kitchen table as if I never cleaned it. Alice whisked eggs in a speckled blue bowl from the back of the cupboard. Three pots sat on the stove, and I smelled Retha's venison chili, warm and pungent. I looked for Mattie.

"She's upstairs with Evelyn," Retha said.

"So it's the entire funeral brigade," I said.

"You should stay away from my father-in-law." Retha laughed, aware that I'd borrowed his nomenclature for their group's culinary response to grief.

Alice grated a chunk of cheese over a casserole filled with macaroni. With slow, long strokes in one direction, she held the cheese between her thumb and two fingers as if the cheese grater could chew up her hand as fast as a combine could grab a sleeve. My mother had handled her domestic duties with this same sense of impending danger, as if to convince me of their significance.

I peeked under the lid to confirm that Retha had brought her venison chili and then said to her, "If you keep packing down the snow with all these visits, I won't have to get out the plow."

"Glad to save you the trouble."

"If you'd called, I could've saved you the trouble of cooking me supper. We ate two hours ago."

"We're not cooking your supper. We're stocking your fridge with meals."

Three full grocery bags from the Supervalu sat on the floor. I had not noticed these, nor the canning jars filled with tomatoes, beets, and cherries. "Retha, I told you to leave me some distractions."

"We don't always know what's best for ourselves," she hesitated, "or others."

"You go on home and let me finish up this good meal you've started. Take all this other food to your families. We're managing just fine."

Alice emptied the grocery bag and grouped the contents on the counter. Corn meal, which I already had, and lasagna noodles, which I never bought. She opened each of my cabinets and finally asked, "Where do you keep your muffin tin?"

I walked past her to the pantry. Bread and muffins were the quickest way to make a meal filling, so on the back of the door I hung pans and tins. Anything I used regularly in my kitchen I hung on nails. It worked well enough in the machine shed, so I brought the habit into the kitchen.

Alice blew on the muffin tin as if her breath made it cleaner than a bit of dust. "You know we have a new young minister. You should join us one week."

"Are you still trying to find me a husband?"

"I said young."

Retha laughed. "You think Alice would set you up with a minister?"

"She'd try anything to save my soul."

My soul and my singleness had given her and my mother ample conversation material for years. These women tried to convince me that I would find joy in marrying and staying indoors. But they could not compete with my father's love for this farm nor his attentive guidance of my brother.

"Did you marry off those boys of yours yet?" I asked.

Retha laughed. "I didn't know you'd gotten so desperate up here by yourself."

"They found fine women," Alice said, more as a reply to Retha than to me.

"What are you looking for, Retha?" I asked.

She had opened and closed nearly every cabinet as we talked. "I know you must have a frying pan."

"Staring right at you." I pointed to the pan hanging over the stove.

"We would have done this in our own kitchens," Retha said, "but I was worried the men would eat it faster than we could finish."

"Lloyd wouldn't touch a crumb if I told him not to." Alice wiped her hands on her apron and poured corn muffin batter into the tin. "We wanted to give you time with Mattie."

Retha glared at Alice. "Or give you time in the barn. You can go back out and let us watch her for a bit."

"No, I'll help in here."

"Go relax." Retha cracked two eggs into a bowl of ricotta cheese.

"Have you ever seen her sit down?" Alice asked, as if I had already left the room.

I wanted to take their advice and read the newspaper while they cooked my supper. But I had worked too hard to suddenly need them, so I emptied the grocery bags.

"You brought enough food for a week."

"We figured it might take time before a Brubaker is able to take the girl," Alice said.

"Actually, Zela wanted me to raise her," I said confidently, though from the moment I found the suitcase I doubted this.

"Of course you must feel obligated to a childhood friend," Alice said.

They made assumptions as quickly as they had when Morris returned married to Charlotte. "We never stopped being friends," I said. I put the oatmeal and the box of raisins back into the Supervalu bag.

"Of course," Retha said as she frowned at Alice. "She didn't mean to imply otherwise." She motioned for me to sit. "You must miss her terribly. Tell us about it."

Alice took the oatmeal out of the bag. "All I'm saying is that no one would think less of you if you gave her to family."

They had not come to bring me supper. They came to set me straight. "I suppose you've already talked about who I should give Mattie to," I said.

"Now, we're not trying to interfere," Retha said.

Alice paused in slicing butter into the bowl. "Do you have anyone in mind?"

"Can't say I thought that far ahead. But Zela's cousin lives in Akron."

"My lands, no. She has six of her own," Retha said.

"Leave it up to the good Lord," Alice said.

"Who do you ladies have in mind?" I suspected they had not planned on telling me directly, but I knew the answer from their hesitation. "Morris," I said.

"What a marvelous idea." Alice clapped her hands. "Not every woman could forgive like you have."

"He is her closest kin," Retha said, as if apologizing for making me say his name. "Family should take care of their own."

"It's been good of you to keep her for a time," Alice said. "Everyone says so."

Their admiration rested on my continuation of what they deemed right. It was the same when my father died. After my father's heart attack, everyone in the valley admired my working the farm. They stopped admiring me when they realized I intended on farming it on my own after he died. The Goswells had sons whom I would not marry nor sell my farm to so they could expand their father's land.

"I'm going to check on Mattie," I said.

"You just leave this to us," Alice said, as she sprinkled raisins into the bowl.

Before I reached the top of the stairs, Retha reprimanded Alice for bringing up Morris before they baked the cookies. In the spare room, Evelyn read a children's book. Her voice rose and fell as if in song. I peeked into the room without their notice. Mattie sat in the crook of Evelyn's arm. Evelyn smiled her overly ambitious smile, which came from either smiling too widely or having large teeth. I never could tell which.

I walked quietly back down the stairs to my office where I would work until they left. I could not blame them. When you believed in a God who climbed into flesh to interrupt history, taking over someone's kitchen could seem caring.

Chapter Six

The creek showed signs of spring. Ice thawed with a warmth perceptible only to those who farmed the valley. Sluggish water rose between blocks of ice though snow continued to fall. Winter, like grieving, was a succession of false endings.

After two weeks I had hardly taught Mattie my basic morning routine. Her complaints filled my accustomed silence of solitary chores. "It's too hard." "It's too heavy." "It takes too long." It was shameful the way the child skittered around work and cold.

The cuckoo sprung from the clock six times, and Mattie ran back to the spare room for a second pair of socks after walking on the cold linoleum. I missed the wood floors covered with rag rugs. After visiting Zela the week Mattie was born, I ordered the same pattern from Sears and Roebuck and laid it myself. It was my one extravagance on the house, and I regretted it.

Mattie clomped down the stairs wearing her snow boots. She took her coat from me but ignored her scarf. "You look old enough to dress yourself," I said, as I coiled the scarf around her neck and face.

"I am," she said, tucking the scarf under her chin and following me into the yard. Tiny snowdrifts gathered as she scooted her feet through them. She trailed to my right, scraping fresh tracks of snow.

"Pick up your feet," I said. She dug her trenches deeper through the snow. I ignored her rather than saying it again. I did not know how to make her obey; I only hoped she would.

The barn gave the impression of warmth with the soft shuffle of cows and the sudden cessation of wind. Work would warm us, even as snowflakes sputtered through cracks between the limestone blocks that supported the barn. Someone had knife-etched "1871" into one of the blocks, as if he knew the date would matter eventually.

Mattie shifted the scarf to cover her nose as I sprayed out two dented buckets and drizzled soap in the bottom. I handed her a rag and a bucket only half-filled with water so she could carry it.

I roped the three cows to a bar over their feeding trough as they crowded over the dusty timothy grass and clover baled in the summer. Their forthright intentions comforted me.

I positioned my stool close to Hannah. "This one's yours," I said to Mattie. I hauled a bale of straw under Willa and sat at an uncomfortable angle to scrub the teats. Mattie patted the udder and the teats with her rag.

"They're not going to drop off," I said. "Clean them right."

Mattie informed me that women never milked cows in her schoolbooks. The cow kicked as I tugged the teat too hard. I became clumsy in a routine no one had watched since I was a child. Even when my father stood over me to see if I followed his instructions, I milked more confidently. Cows sensed incompetence. Children were no different.

Swiping the rag at the brown sludge that spackled the udder, Mattie asked, "What is it?"

"Mud. Manure. Just clean it." I squirted the warm milk into the sanitized bucket. Now buckets were described as sanitized, when in my father's day a clean bucket would do.

"Yuck. Yuck." Mattie chanted as she lightly rubbed the rag under the udder. This was progress. I had bribed her from the doorway to the stool to finally touching the cow. If she milked the cow, I would buy her milk at the Supervalu. It was watery milk that slid so quickly over the tongue it had no taste. A waste of a dollar. But Mattie claimed she tasted cow in my milk.

The barn cat that hid from Mattie ran to the door at the sound of Stanley's whistle. Stanley had a purposeful cheerfulness around the child. He came by the barn earlier in the mornings, yet in the time I usually milked three cows on my own, we only milked two. He seemed to expect leniency from his work now that a child distracted me.

I rarely kept a hired man long after he relaxed. I learned this from one man who had relaxed enough to believe he could grab me from behind as I worked in the barn, as entitled to me as the land he worked. Swinging the first object I could grasp, I stunned him with the slap of an old horse bridle. I saw none of this man in Stanley's eyes, but I kept watch for it.

A draft of snow and wind followed Stanley through the door. Stepping over the calico cat, he walked directly to Mattie and shook his snow-covered head over her. "Brr," he said.

"Stanley." She giggled and genteelly brushed off her arms.

I scooted closer to the cow and glared at Stanley as he walked toward me. His jacket was still covered in snow. "Don't even think of it," I said.

He turned as though he would walk away and then flapped his arms, showering the remaining snow on me.

"Stanley," I yelled. Mattie stopped laughing as I brushed myself off and shook the snow from my hair.

"Seems you prefer play to work lately." I stood and handed him an empty bucket. "Remind me why you're useful." I jerked my head toward Mattie to divert his intense stare. "Want to show her again?"

"Little one," he said in the singsong voice Evelyn used to read to Mattie, as if children heard music before words, "what did I say yesterday?" He tapped his forefinger to his thumb, tapping a rhythm for his swaying steps.

"Pinch at the top," Mattie said.

"Yes," he said excitedly and tapped his forefinger and thumb in mini-applause. He had an ease with Mattie that made me wonder if he had left children of his own in Germany.

Mattie pinched her fingers at the fleshy joint near the udder.

"One finger at a time. Squish out the milk," Stanley coached. "Again. Spread your fingers." Mattie pinched again and pressed each finger toward her hand. A squirt of milk sprayed onto the straw-covered floor. Stanley clapped for Mattie who smiled wide-eyed at him.

"Save the clapping," I said. No one learned by applause. He would only slow her down with the belief that she had already succeeded. I learned this from my father who said little of small accomplishments. He said nothing of my larger accomplishments either, believing that the reward lay in the completion of the task.

The short beeps of a car horn sent Mattie to the door before I had time to stand.

"Who is it?"

Mattie shrugged and ran back toward Stanley. "Show me again." His instructions differed little from mine, and yet here she sat, squeezing milk into the bucket. I grabbed my jacket from a nail and told them to try to finish milking the cows before their next feeding.

Uncle Charlie drove his 1948 Plymouth slowly toward the barn. New cars were no longer the fashion in his age group. He slowly pulled into the turnaround at the side of the barn, and I looked in the passenger seat for my cousin, whom Charlie had threatened to bring, but he was alone.

I walked down the middle of the drive from the barn to the house, so that his car crept behind me. Charlie had a nine-to-five sensibility that brought him at the same time on the same day every three months. He never called before his visits, and he never came unexpectedly.

I poured myself a cup of lukewarm coffee to occupy my hands and waited by the door as Charlie struggled to climb from his car. Typically I had more time to steady myself for his visits. I felt a fear older than my memories.

Charlie tucked his cane over one arm and balanced himself with both hands on the railing to climb the steps.

He opened the door, and I held it open without backing up.

"Sometimes your elders need a hand."

"You're too early for a payment."

"Do you have enough for two?" he asked, as he pointed to my coffee cup.

"Our days start earlier out here. It's the middle of my day, and I have better things to do than drink coffee with you."

"It's always a pleasure to see you, Dottie. You're the only person I know who starts fighting before she knows what she's fighting about."

With a slight nudge to my shoulder, he walked purposefully to my kitchen table. "Were you with your father when he died?"

I followed him to the table, understanding his ability to intimidate came from his habit of success. "You should have asked me fourteen years ago." I wondered if he remembered what he actually said at the burial. As we walked away from my father's grave, he offered to relieve my mother and me of the burden of the farm, and we talked business for the first time. Ten feet from my father's grave, I negotiated my first contract with Charlie. "He said nothing of you, if that's what you're getting at," I said.

"So you were with him. As it should be," he sighed. "It's all a parent can ask for in those final hours."

"There's nothing about death that should be. Makes little difference now that I was with him. I'm the one left with the memory."

"And a clear conscience."

"He wouldn't want to be remembered the way I remember him."

"But he's remembered."

"You didn't come to talk about my father."

"Perhaps not," Charlie said, as he took off his coat and folded his cashmere scarf in a neat square. "Or perhaps everything we discuss involves your father."

"I paid you for this quarter, and daylight is slipping past me." I got up from the table.

Charlie waited until I reached for my jacket to tell me the reason he had come. "I intend to give the farm to my son."

I hung the coat on the peg, taking care to loop the tag over the hook. I thought no further than that act. I joined him at the table. "Start talking."

"I offered the farm to any of my children who would take it. I want them near me."

"You'd lose money. Not one of them has farmed a day in his life."

He waved his hand as one accustomed to dismissing ideas before hearing them. "This valley is always a dollar short. And I have money. There are plenty of boys to hire. Your cousin Rex accepted my offer."

"We have an agreement."

"One you should read closer." Charlie struggled to stand. He balanced himself between the chair and the counter as he tipped his hat before securing it on his puff of hair. "Rex arrives in two weeks. He'll want to move in by spring."

I waited until his car door slammed before I walked onto the porch. When he still worked for Farmer's First National, Charlie had foreclosed two farms in the valley because they did not believe his threats as I did. Some slow years I bargained better than others, but I always bargained until Charlie drew up another contract for me to sign. I sucked in a quick breath at the realization that this time Charlie's threat had not been about money. I stood on the porch long after his car left the lane.

Chapter Seven

The Lutherans were the first to stake out the corner of Main Street and Brubaker Avenue as holy ground. The Brubakers hired a bricklayer from Mansfield for the task. These farmers, who unearthed limestone for the foundations of their barns and homes and felled walnut and pine for the beams, shipped in bricks kilned in the East and hired others to build their churches. By the turn of the century four churches sat within two blocks of one another, and a safe ten-minute drive from my farm.

"I heard church bells," Mattie announced Sunday morning. She came into the living room dressed as if it were Easter. She twirled to show me the gift from Morris and Charlotte, an impractical dress with rows of lace covering the pale lavender fabric and a deep purple sash hanging untied. Last Tuesday evening, we came into the house from the barn to find a dress and shampoo on the kitchen table and a note written in Charlotte's handwriting on a torn piece of graph paper. The large, bold loops of her letters reminded me of the curls in her red hair. We had never met, yet when I first glimpsed her with Morris I noticed her hair. I ripped the jagged remainder of the graph paper from the pad and balled it with the note to throw in the trash. Morris should not have brought her here.

Yet here Mattie stood with her hair smelling of the perfumed lilac shampoo, reminding me of Charlotte's visit. Clean was more convincing without a smell.

I tossed another log onto the fire, sending a spray of firefly sparks above the flames. She had smoothed her drying hair in the front to clip on blue plastic, butterfly barrettes. The back was wet and tangled. The tangles suggested she did not have a mirror or a mother.

"You couldn't have heard them," I told her. The bells could only be heard in town. I eased back in my reading chair and opened my accounting books. I spent the morning confirming the results of last year's rainy spring, which delayed planting by three weeks. I accumulated and lost my small savings as regularly as Alice had grandchildren. This past year I spent my savings to cover expenses that the crops had not begun to pay. Late into the night, I reread my contract with Charlie. He held the deed until the final payment, a condition I had known but not fully grasped until last night. I could not claim partial ownership—a point Charlie always refused to negotiate.

"They sounded close." Mattie took kid gloves from the front pocket of her dress.

"It's no closer than the school, and you never hear its bell in the morning," I said to distract her with our most recent argument. Every morning that I drove her to school, Mattie refused to get out of the truck. I agreed with Zela's cousin in Akron who suggested Mattie stay with me until the end of the school year. Though she had not yet proposed the idea to her husband, she called to tell me Mattie needed parents and was sure they could do something.

"Church always starts at ten-thirty. We're going to be late." She brushed her gloved hand over her cheek to smooth back bangs that needed to be trimmed. I had not considered in years what time church began. God was as distant as a grandparent who died in my childhood. I remembered Him as liking quiet children best and daughters who wore dresses and smiled often. He wanted us to sit up straight and not laugh too loudly. He and my mother seemed to agree on most things until my brother died.

"We're not going."

"Why not?"

I had worked out plenty of reasons to tell others why I stopped attending church, but it had been fourteen years since those conversations. Only Alice persisted in inviting me, and she'd grown accustomed to me simply refusing her without reasons. How could I tell Mattie that the hymns they sang and sermons they heard never mentioned the God I experienced? The God I prayed to took away the very things I asked for. When I was left with only the farm, I knew I would never pray for His help to keep it. I preferred taking my chances with my own efforts, yet I had not mustered up enough faith to stop believing in Him entirely.

When I did not answer her, she said, "It's Sunday." She turned and waved a sash in each hand for me to tie. She argued like her Uncle Morris, casually, without the thought of losing.

"Which isn't any different from Monday or Tuesday. You might as well change your clothes."

She waited with her arms crossed, watching me. I studied the figures in my account book, but never wrote a single figure or made any sense from the columns of numbers that divided the page like a well-plowed field. She waited until the cuckoo whistled the quarter hour and then the half hour. At eleven, she left the room. I shut the book. My eyes ached from their stillness. I rested my head against the back of the chair. It would have taken less energy to pin on a hat and drive to the Methodist Church.

Stanley had not saved his first week's earnings for a carving knife or for a new hat. He bought six cans of Silver Fleece sauerkraut, three cans of red sockeye salmon, and four cans of Bell's pitted firm olives, which I saw in the pile of tins. I never cooked with salmon or olives, but I could tolerate sauerkraut. For our noon meal that Sunday, I cooked a pork roast smothered in it. I dished up Stanley's meal first and covered it with another plate to keep it warm until he came for it. I scraped the sauerkraut from Mattie's pork and set her plate at the table. Before I could dish up my own supper, Mattie took her plate and Stanley's.

"I'm going to eat with Stanley," she said. She balanced both plates and walked to the door expectantly. She could not open the door holding both plates.

"Don't make a habit of it." I held the screen door open and allowed her to pass under my arm. I had refused her enough in one day and liked the thought of eating alone in my reading chair by the fire rather than propped up at the table.

As I ate I read the latest *Farm Journal.* I drifted to sleep writing a letter to the editor, who blamed the increased mechanization of farming for the deaths of children. Forestalling death wasn't as simple as that. My brother had accepted a dare to walk the highest beam in the barn. Neither Morris nor Zela nor I could blame the other for the dare; we had all agreed to it and all expected to follow. It happened that my brother volunteered to go first.

I gradually woke at the sound of Morris's laughter in my kitchen. I could not have remembered his laugh if asked, but I knew it as soon as I heard him. He had a deep laugh that he never hid. His confident laugh gave others courage to laugh loudly with him. Mattie giggled in response to something he said.

I had slept for nearly two hours. I rubbed my face, embarrassed by the dampness of drool on my cheek. I had slept too soundly and wondered if I snored, something Mattie recently informed me she heard through the wall. Fluffing my hair with my fingers, I knew without a mirror I looked worn and rumpled. I pressed my lips together for color, an instinctual response from high school that I had forgotten, and then smoothed my flannel shirt over my jeans before going into the kitchen.

Mattie was asking Morris if he had watched "Anything Can Happen Day," her favorite day, she told him, on the Mickey Mouse show. She sighed and said it had been weeks and weeks since she had seen it.

"You should have woke me," I said, as I walked into the kitchen.

"You obviously needed the rest." He spoke with such care that for a moment I was too tired to fight the desire to come near him. I grasped the back of the chair instead.

"Look what Uncle Morris brought me," Mattie exclaimed, holding out another dress.

"Looks the same as the dress this morning," I said.

"That one didn't have flowers." She showed me the imprint of tulips that streaked the dress like sunlight. She ran to the bathroom to try it on. I would find her work clothes heaped on the floor tonight.

"She has no place to wear them."

Morris nodded as if that was the reason he bought them.

After a few minutes, Mattie ran into the kitchen. "It's perfect," she announced. "I'm going to show Stanley." The dress flared under her when she sat on the floor to pull on her boots.

"Not without long johns. Your legs will fall off in this cold," I said.

"I'll be right back." The door slammed behind her. Her mittens flapped on the string that ran through her coat sleeves. Her knit hat lay on the floor.

"Call after her." Morris stood from the table. "It's only ten degrees."

"Which will bring her back quicker than a minute," I said. "She's old enough to know when her legs get too cold. Besides, the workroom's heated."

"Is it as drafty as this house?" He sat down and drummed his fingers on the table.

"Draftier," I said, "which is why she has no use for those dresses. It only makes it harder to convince her to wear her work clothes."

"What work could she possibly do?"

"The same work we did as children," I said. "She's learned to milk a cow."

Morris stood and paced the length of the kitchen. He fidgeted with the buttons on his sleeves, seeming to need a yellow legal pad to occupy his hands while he made his case. The city paid him to argue. This amused me.

"She needs to return to school."

"Spending a few weeks learning how the world works can't hurt her."

"Your world, Dottie. Mattie will marry and buy her milk at a grocery store."

This had been the extent of my mother's hope for me. She believed a man who could provide bottled milk delivered to her door would have far surpassed my father, who asked her to can enough fruits and vegetables in the summer to sustain our family throughout the year.

"Maybe so, but the boys aren't proposing in second grade, so it shouldn't hurt her chances." Then I offered coffee in hopes of distracting him from what I had said.

He shook his head no, apparently not aware of the memory that settled on me. When I was not much older than Mattie, I took a hoe into the woods to clear a path that diverged from my brother's. Morris came looking for my brother and walked along my path instead. As we talked, I hacked away at saplings and sumac. He followed behind me, tossing the cut brush into the woods. Deep in the woods, he said, "After we get married, I'll build us a cabin back here." I promised to clear the land for our farm. Had Zela or Samuel been with us or had we walked in a familiar part of the forest, either of us could have easily melted into giggles. But our work of clearing the forest made us momentary adults. After his actual proposal we walked the woods looking for the path, but May apples covered our tracks.

"My cousin called me," he said. "She says you're trying to pass off Mattie to her."

"I thought it would be good for Mattie to be with other children."

"But not with her aunt and uncle in a familiar town," he said.

"I haven't made any decisions," I said, which was true now that the cousin had proven herself untrustworthy.

Morris stared out the window overlooking the fields. "You've done well for yourself. No one thought you'd keep this place running on your own." I ignored him, knowing that in the next breath he would make me regret accepting his compliment. "I don't see how you can do all of this and raise a daughter on your own."

"Charlotte and I live ten minutes from her school," he said. "Mattie needs a family with a father and a mother who has time to mother her," he paused. The refrigerator clicked and hummed in our silence. "She needs someone who will take her to church."

"Why do you assume she doesn't go to church?" I asked.

Then I learned of the phone calls. Mattie made them from the machine shed when I was in the house.

"She calls Charlotte to cry," Morris said.

I imagined her working the stubborn, rusted latch of the shed. I saw her clearing a spot on the workbench so she could climb onto it, as she did the kitchen counters, to reach the phone. I wanted to shoo Morris from the house and call for Mattie. I would simply hold her.

Then another, more familiar, feeling swept through me when I remembered the party line. Every woman in the valley knew of her calls. I knew now why they had come with food. I was surprised by the intensity of the anger and the sudden memory of when my mother called Alice to tell her that Morris had married Charlotte. I could not have hidden this from anyone, but she also told Alice that he never broke our engagement. Both Mattie and my mother were weak. It took strength to keep family business where it belonged.

"What do you want?" I asked.

"We want to adopt Mattie. We're her family."

"Don't bring your wife back to this house, and I'll think about it."

There was a way things were done in the valley, a way in which I believed. A family should take care of their own. She could attend a school where she could wear her dresses, the lavender dress with the flowers and the lavender dress without the flowers. They could afford to spoil her in ways I could not, even if I had money.

By nightfall, I knew what I would say to Mattie about using the workroom phone. I would begin with words, telling her that no one should know our family business, and then I would use the wooden spoon that my mother had used on me. When I called for her, she yelled from the bathroom that she would come in a minute.

When she did not come, I climbed the stairs two at a time. Mattie stood on a stool in front of the bathroom mirror. Every brush and comb that I owned was piled on the bathroom counter. One side of her hair hung straight. She had the other side in two handfuls, trying to twist them together. She had a rubber band between her teeth.

"I called for you, Matilda Ann."

She spit the rubber band onto the counter. "If I let go, it unravels."

When the tears came, she shrugged her shoulder toward her cheek to brush them away. She held tight to the two strands of hair. "I always wore braids." She sucked in deep breaths to stop the crying. I watched her reflection in the mirror and admired her ability to make the tears disappear.

"It takes three strands," I said softly. Zela had braided Mattie's hair in two braids on each side and tied them with matching ribbons. When she was a girl, she had done the same with her doll, Bitsy. Bitsy went to school with us, tucked under her arm. I attended Bitsy's funeral, when Zela's mother declared the doll infected with Zela's measles. A solemn Zela laid the blanket-wrapped doll in the ground. I never understood her love for the doll, but I tossed a handful of daisies on the mound and said her beauty would always be remembered.

I chose a brush from the two on the counter and tucked a rat-tail comb in my shirt pocket. "Did any of the girls at your school wear French braids?"

She told me of one girl, whose mother owned the beauty shop. She stopped when I tried to loosen the tangled strands from her hand.

"Sit on the toilet," I said. "And I'll French braid it."

She let go of the strands that quickly loosened from her attempts to wind them together.

I had only braided my hair and Zela's. Zela had a picture book to teach us. I told Mattie this as I brushed the tangles from her hair. I learned and gave Zela a French braid for her first date. Not to be outdone, Zela practiced until I had a single fishbone braid down my back. It took hours, and she never attempted it again.

"Why did you cut your hair?"

"More practical this way," I said.

She craned her head back and looked at me. "I bet it was pretty."

I touched the back of my neck, naked of hair. The home-perm kept the hair in tight curls. I rarely ever thought of it. "It was," I said.

Her hair was as soft as corn silk. The bathroom smelled of damp towels. The air was warm and close from Mattie's bath. I twisted the strands of hair between my fingers. I took my time, smoothing each strand, checking the sides to keep them even, but still I finished too quickly.

I wound the rubber band around the end and told her to never use the workroom phone. "Everyone along this road can listen. And you don't want everyone to hear you cry, do you?" Mattie shook her head.

"It looks very pretty," I said, as I handed her the mirror.

Chapter Eight

Only two weeks after I spoke with Charlie, his son, Rex, drove a 1962 Ford F-100 pickup into town. Fords of every color and year stirred dirt between the valley and Mansfield. Not a farmer in the valley could afford to buy them new, and Rangoon Red was a new color by our standards. We owned Woodsmoke Gray and Goldenrod Yellow, colors our gas attendant made it his business to know. He identified the make and model by the color and, soon, so did everyone in the valley. My 1954 was Sea Haze Green. A 1962 Rangoon Red was impractical.

I was in the spare room when I saw the truck parked on the road in front of my farm, but I continued my work. I carried another armful of boxes into my parents' old room. White sheets covered the furniture like snow banks that never thawed. I dragged the boxes from the closet in the spare room and then stacked them in the corner of my parents' room. My mother had wanted to dispose of these boxes before my father died, before it would be disrespectful. But I would not let her.

Mattie could not live out of a suitcase until I made a decision, and she needed a closet. My father's boxes crowded the corner of the room. One was labeled "Good Soles," another simply "Seeds."

After I stacked the last box in the corner, the red truck was still parked in front of my farm. Unknown cars rarely traveled our road. I went into the living room to get a direct look at the truck and to listen to any talk on the party line.

Evelyn Yates was describing the truck when I picked up the line. "Lord, have mercy, if any of our husbands see that truck."

The truck exhaled a steady stream of exhaust as a man walked the edge of the field. He wore a gray Stetson. His hands were jammed in the pockets of a hunting jacket that had never seen a tree stand. He had a vague resemblance to my cousin, who left Mansfield to find work acting in motion picture shows when he was eighteen years old.

"He told Lloyd he came to farm the Connell land," Alice said, always one to offer details. "Said he's Dottie's cousin."

"Dottie would never sell," Evelyn said.

"That's the question now. Some say the land might not be hers to sell," Alice said. Retha knew the truth and said nothing. I blessed her under my breath.

"How could that be . . ." Evelyn paused, "Dottie, are you listening?"

"Not to anything good." I sat on the arm of my couch.

"We've told you before. Tell us when you come on," Alice said.

"Planned to when one of you took a breath."

"Why is he here?" Retha asked.

"Can't a boy visit?"

"What's this talk of him coming to farm your land?" Alice asked.

"Just talk." I brushed the dust off of my shirt in case Rex came down my drive. He did not, and I listened to the women as the truck left my sight.

"Lord, have mercy, if they see that truck."

I ran my hand along the tires of the Cat, cracked like the creek in a drought. I checked the carcass for breaks and listened to Stanley talk to a tractor as if he eased a bit into a horse's mouth. He had a way with animals and children that he had not found with machines.

He stood back from the 1940 John Deere tractor as if distance provided the perspective he needed. I hated the overpriced tractor purchased by my father after he lost his heart for farming and absorbed debt like a man with no heirs.

"The gasket and washers are replaced," Stanley said. Without Mattie to entertain, Stanley settled back to our way of talking. I relaxed. It was gruff and purposeful. In these tones we would discuss machines and fertilizers. We would accomplish something with our talk, and I could forget the decisions I had to make.

"You over-inflated the tires of the Cat."

"Bigger problem here." He pointed to the tractor. An oil-stained rag hung as testimony from his front jeans pocket. "The oil has quarts of water in it. I cannot find the leak."

I nodded and picked up the belt from the other supplies he had bought at Pete's Hardware in town and walked over to the mower. He wasn't asking for advice, and I would not have insulted him by giving it. After my father died, I fixed every machine in the shed by watching Mr. Hilliard and reading, not from asking. I popped open the hood of the mower and slipped on my gloves.

Stanley followed me to the other side of the shed. "What do you think?"

"Don't you want to figure it out?"

"It saves the time to ask."

"It's winter. We have time."

"You think I'm weak for asking." He raised his eyebrows, creasing his broad forehead. I had seen this expression when he bargained with the man who overpriced parts at the implement store in Ashland. He raised his eyebrows when he knew he was right.

"Yes," I said. "If you find the leak, you'll find it the next time."

"Something else could cause the leak the next time."

"Not likely. But you learn what to look for."

"And what to avoid?" He raised his eyebrows again, as if to emphasize that he wasn't talking about the tractor.

I walked over to the tractor. "Have you checked the push rod tubes?"

"Yes."

"Did you drill any exhaust manifold studs?"

He nodded. I paused, hating to point out the obvious answer. He looked at the tractor and shrugged his shoulders.

"Any ideas?" I asked.

"This is why I asked you. You know this machine," he said.

"You should figure out this tractor before you think you know me," I said. "You probably drilled too deep."

Stanley folded his arms and leaned back on the tool bench. This man, so playful with Mattie, folded into a silence that distracted me. I pulled the valve rocker shaft and the push rods. A wrench hung from the side of Stanley's tool belt that I motioned for, and he handed it to me. He crouched beside me as I loosened the tire bolts and watched me intently. "Study the push rod tubes if you want to learn something."

We jacked up the tractor and removed the front wheels. As we eased the front of the tractor onto the floor, Stanley asked, "Who is the man who visits?"

"Mattie's uncle." The tractor knelt like a crippled horse. It had the wounded smell of gasoline. I filled the shaft and the rod with water. "Watch for water coming out of the tubes and you'll find the leak," I said.

"This I already know."

"Then why did you ask?"

"Not the tractor, the man. I know he is Mattie's uncle, but he is more than this?"

"An old friend."

"More, I think."

"Where are you getting the time to come up with these ideas?" He never talked so freely with me. Mattie had loosened his tongue. "Should I find more work to keep you busy?"

"Would more work mean that I could stay?"

"You know I don't promise more than a season of work."

"But with Mattie, you need more help."

"I may not keep her," I said. He nodded, as if he expected my answer. "Crawl under that tractor and make yourself useful. Look for the water leak."

The tractor belly covered his head. His jeans were scuffed with dirt and his blue and gray flannel was stiff from drying on a line in his room. He waited for the water, which I knew was minutes from trickling through the tubes. Working with Mattie, I had missed this work where one could test for answers.

"Her uncle wants her," I said. Then, barely loud enough for myself to hear, I asked, "What do you think of that?"

From the silence, I assumed Stanley could not hear me under the tractor. Then he said, "Do what's best for the girl."

I knelt and peered under the machine. A small trickle of water revealed the leak. "It's not every day I ask advice. Might help if you say it straight out."

"You don't want her," he said.

"Look at that," I said pointing his attention to the leak. "You'll need to replace the studs." I crawled away from the tractor and shoved myself back to my feet. "Put the replacements in the freezer tonight. It will make it easier to drive them in tomorrow," I said, realizing my error in asking advice from a man who could not find a water leak in a tractor. How could he know what I wanted when I did not know myself?

He offered me the rag before wiping his hands. The oil stained the lines in my hands as I wiped off the excess. As he studied my face, I felt our nearness. He reached toward me as if he would stroke my cheek. I smacked his hand. "Oil," he said quickly. "You have oil on your face."

He appeared stunned for a moment, and then left the shed faster than I could call after him to tell him he had merely startled me.

Chapter Nine

In the two days after Rex drove his truck into town, I imagined our meeting too many times to wait for it. To change his plans, I needed to know them. I had bargained fourteen years with his father to keep my land. I needed to find out Rex's price. From the talk on the party line, I knew he already had a habit of evenings at the Red Onion.

After settling Mattie in bed and asking Stanley to keep an eye toward the house, I drove to the Red Onion. I drove past it at first, remembering it hidden at the end of a dirt path marked by two spruce pines on either side. I passed a floodlit, wooden sign with a red onion etched next to the bar's name. I parked beside Rex's truck.

On the glass door, a plastic sign posted the hours written neatly in preprinted boxes. This was not the two-room shanty of twenty years ago, from which men were thrown through a wooden door to cool off in the quiet of the woods. Then it hadn't needed a floodlit sign, but operated by word of mouth that good folks shouldn't be seen there but often were.

Before my mother died, I had drunk whiskey and played poker here on Saturday nights. It was the least complicated way for a woman to sin and the easiest way to worry my mother. When my soul needed saving, she had less time to write to her friends in Erie to find me a husband.

Now matching black vinyl booths and stools furnished the Red Onion. The only similarities to the old hangout were the fusty smell of beer sloshed onto the wood floor and the foggy air. Men at the bar looked toward the television suspended from one of the pine beams running across the ceiling. At the bar, Rex occupied the bartender in conversation. The bar was made of walnut, varnished to a high shine, which was a far cry from yellow pine planks supported by apple crates. Everyone in the bar was my age. The younger people must have met in other woods, where they believed they could dream up sins more interesting than those of their parents.

I sat at a shadowed side booth where I could see the length of the bar. A soft haze of cigarette smoke floated in the dim lighting over the mirror. Rex's reflection moved into sight for brief moments of his animated tales. I ordered what was on tap, and I ordered for Rex whatever he was drinking. The waitress asked, "Should I tell him it's from you, Dottie?"

I had not recognized her in the dim light. She graduated a few years after me in school. It still surprised me to see people younger than myself looking middle-aged.

"Tell him it's from a woman."

After I ordered a second drink for Rex, he balanced his gray Stetson on his head and walked toward me with his drink in hand.

"I like to meet women who try to get me drunk." He smiled winningly.

I moved so the light of the bar shone on my face. "Howdy, cousin."

"If it isn't my Aunt Louise."

"I hope that's the gin talking."

"Aunt Louise wasn't much of a drinker, so you must be Dottie." I scowled at the second mention of my mother. As he slid his hat across the table to rest near the napkin holder, he held out his hand, which was bread-dough soft.

I nodded toward his hat. "Come a bit too far East?"

He smiled. "I've always wanted a hat like this." Rex had his mother's face, which was too pretty for a man, and his mother's stoutness, which was allowed on a man.

He waved the waitress over to order a late supper. He had spent the day exploring Carson, the closest town to the valley, and he had forgotten to eat. He stopped in the feed mill, Connie's Clip and Curl, Pete's Hardware, the Valley Restaurant, and Farmer's First National and was surprised everyone knew his father.

I listened as I would to prepare for an approaching storm, counting the seconds from bolt to thunder. I watched him as I would watch leaves to learn the direction of the wind.

He talked of California, using the phrase that had scattered the children of the valley after the war, "You should see." But they would never truly see another place until they saw their own land with freckled mushrooms after rain or pink tear drops on white apple blossoms in the spring. As Rex described California with its neon and movie stars, I knew he would never really see my land.

He told me of his wife and his mistress, his wife's best friend, who in the end preferred their friendship to him. He reminisced about his childhood times on my farm. This past had never occurred, yet he remembered it as if it had. He recalled playing hide-and-seek in the cornfield and fishing in our pond. I did not tell him my memories of sitting in our Uncle Charlie's dining room on stiff-backed chairs until Samuel and I apologized for leaving our wailing cousins in the cornfield or for jumping from the canoe with the paddles and abandoning them in the middle of the pond.

The waitress delivered two platter plates, one with fried chicken, the other piled with onion rings. She put down a jar of mayonnaise and took away the bottles of mustard and ketchup. Rex smiled. "Good memory."

He jabbed a pile of onion rings with his fork and quartered them with a steak knife. He crunched a mouthful of them, licked his fingers, and then cut the chicken off the bone in the same manner.

"Every day we think we're making choices. Which way to drive home, which toothpaste to buy, which woman to love. But life has this terrible tendency. If you stop watching it for a moment," Rex lathered the chunks of chicken with mayonnaise as he spoke, "only a moment, it slips into the mundane."

I sipped my beer. "A few beers in this place can make you feel you understand things."

"No, it's not just this place. I thought about this long before I drove across the country. Choices make us feel alive. I needed to feel alive."

"Farming will do that. Nothing like being alive at six in the morning when it's two degrees."

"It will be good to get away from it all."

"What all are you wanting to get away from?"

"The rush of everything. People."

"Neighbors can live so close together they don't want to know one another. People here care so much about one another, it occupies all of their conversations."

He talked of the imagined satisfaction of working with his hands and seeing the fruit of his labor. I waved for the waitress and asked for ketchup and another platter of onion rings.

As I ate, I considered why he had come and ways to make him leave. When I had savings, I kept it in cash, locked in a vault under my father's oak business desk. My safe only held the ledger of neatly written figures and five hundred dollars. Over the past few evenings I had worked up figures based on crops that surpassed my expected profits.

"You have a girl. Was it with that fellow you always ran with?" Rex asked.

"No. She's not mine. I'm keeping her for a time."

In this season of beards, Rex sprouted October stubble that he stroked as though he had February growth. He told me I deserved more. The girl deserved more. Scraping together rent to pay his father was not the way to live. Sometimes outsiders could show us how to do better for ourselves, he concluded.

"What did your father make you promise to keep you tied to that farm, all alone, this long?" he asked.

"No promise is stronger than one we make with ourselves," I said. "I'll give you five hundred dollars to give up your crazy idea. It's plenty of money to find something else to make you feel alive."

Rex chuckled. "That wouldn't pay off my plane fare, the truck I bought to drive here, and the clothes on my back."

"I can give you seven thousand next fall," I said, rashly. "It's more than you could make on the farm in the next few years."

Rex drank the last bit of his gin and tonic. He waved over the waitress to order another and told her I had drunk enough to stop talking sensibly. I ordered another beer, though my stomach clenched, and I feared I might lose everything I put in it that evening.

"It doesn't make good business sense for either of us," he said.

"If I based my decisions about this farm on my pocketbook, I wouldn't live there. I'll give you two thousand now. You won't have lost any money, and I'll send more in the fall than you would make struggling with this farm for the next few years."

This moment had always existed in the corner of my eye. I refused to look directly at the lack of documents, which contradicted the feeling that came from walking, loving, working, and tending a land. And for the first time, I wondered who I would be without it. Even if Pete had a moment of profound sympathy and hired me at the hardware store, he would not endure the long-term ribbing he'd get for hiring a woman. If the Hilliards took pity, their farm could not support another person as opinionated as Mr. Hilliard. At best I would travel outside our valley to larger farms looking for work, having less luck than Stanley.

"What's your price, Rex?"

He wiped his mouth with a napkin that was wrinkled and stained with the grease of the meal. "I want to move in by spring. A month should be a fair amount of time for you to find another place."

I waved away the cigarette smoke from the booth behind us. Though I needed outdoor air, I leaned farther across the table. "I'm not leaving my farm. How much money do you want to make this trip worth your while?"

"It's not your farm, Dottie. You need to make plans to leave."

Since my father's death, I had not unlocked his gun cabinet. The cabinet was etched with a scene of grand mountains and a ten-point buck opposite a hunter with perfect form. It sat in the corner of my parents' bedroom. The recently stacked boxes of my father's belongings blocked the front of the cabinet. In a frenzy, I dragged boxes away from the cabinet and piled them in the middle of the room. Sweat swam like tadpoles down my back and into the waistband of my jeans. The exertion displaced the rage that sent me from the Red Onion. Smells puffed into the room as I heaved box upon box. Pipe tobacco. Pond water. Leather. There were fifteen boxes in all. When I finished, I was chilled by the sudden clarity of my thoughts. I would lose my farm.

Behind the glass door, five Remington rifles stood between wooden pegs. My grandmother had been known to shoot with dead accuracy, never raising it from her hip. I knew my instinct to use them to be outdated and unlawful, yet it was an instinct all the same. I imagined sitting on my porch with a rifle across my lap, firing a warning shot toward the sky when they came to take my home. One warning shot to say that I would not leave easily. It brought strength to realize I could do it and comfort to know I would not. They would lock me in a room smaller than Stanley's if I did. We lived in modern times, when people settled for an overpriced half acre. No one outside the valley would understand a woman waving a rifle for three hundred acres.

With my father's belongings piled in the middle of the room, I could not turn in a full circle but was confined to the space between the wall and the gun cabinet. I needed air. The bedroom window groaned as I rocked it open. The cold air tasted as clear and crisp as spring water in the summer.

My father watched me farm from this window after his first stroke left him face down in the field, his cheek pockmarked from pebbles by the time I found him. He called me to this window to point out the ragged edges of the first fields that I plowed. He told me that we would not buy seed the following winter. He planned to use the money to move us to Erie. But by then I had more strength, or at least more desire to be strong, so I spent the money on seed before he bought our train tickets. The mere talk of leaving weakened him more than his stroke. It would have killed him to leave his land. My mother said it would kill him to work a farm he could never own. When he died shortly after, my mother and I each blamed the other.

A week before my mother's death, after my uncle had come for another payment we could not afford, my mother said Charlie could drive anyone to the grave. I had collapsed on the couch after working past ache to a numbness that made me clumsy. She sat next to me and I took her hand that had gone soft with age. It was a rare, tender moment of agreement. But it had ended as quickly as my light squeeze of her fingers when I told her that I would get the farm back.

She tugged on the rope I used to keep my father's overalls around my hips. She had a habit of tugging or dusting off clothing she disapproved of. My mother disapproved of nothing more than my relationship with Morris until that night when she contradicted every plea for me to leave him. She knelt beside me with a jar of Pond's cold cream and took my hand in hers. She worked it into my cracked hands, rubbing the cream deep into the calluses.

Then she said if I had carried myself like a woman, Morris would not have gone off and found another one. "At least with him, you would have had children and lived on a farm more prosperous than this one. I wanted so much more for you." If my father had only kept record of his payments and if all of my profits had not been handed over to Charlie, I would have prospered this farm and proven my mother wrong.

I drank in another breath of cool air. A fresh snowfall mirrored the light of the full moon. The crisp shell of unbroken snow mounds obscured every lane and road. I reached for a box: "Seeds." I knew this box and its contents. Every year my father tucked seeds into an envelope and labeled it with the name of the field where he had planted them. They were the history of this farm and of my father's life on this land. I thumbed through the box. His handwriting was meticulous. He had never missed a year.

I ached at the sight of his boxy handwriting and the inconsistency of it all. He was a cautious man. He would puff on his pipe and stare out the window a full five minutes before answering a question. He would put a letter in the mailbox and open the box a second time to make sure it had a stamp in the corner. He was not the sort of man to lose track of a debt and forfeit his farm because of it. It was as if he wanted Charlie to take the land from me.

My father's boxes crowded around me. This insignificant clutter told me no more about him than he had in his lifetime. I grabbed the first box behind me and threw it out the window. I opened the box labeled "good soles" and flung boots that stepped haphazard footprints in the snow and hurled the box after them. I tossed the box labeled "Tobacco for a Rainy Day" that left my father's smell in the room.

Every time Charlie demanded payment, my father had paid, trusting Charlie's records of compound interest and debt. He kept no records. I flung his ball caps one at a time. They shot from the window and drifted in the wind. I opened each box, shaking his neatly packed collections until they spread across the lawn beneath the window. Banjo trotted into the light of the window. He ran after moth-eaten shirts "needing buttons" and barked at them as they caught wind and stuck in the larch pine. He caught my father's Sunday hat, growled and slapped it back and forth, as if he had caught one of the red-tailed hawks he chased after as they glided over the fields.

An unlabeled box remained in the middle of the room. Its contents did not fit my father's precise division of objects but appeared to be dumped from a desk drawer. I moved newspaper clippings aside to find a fistful of dried daisies that crumbled to dust at my touch. A ripped corner of a quilt with calico squares instantly reminded me of the quilt that Morris and I kept hidden under hay bales in the barn. I rubbed the fabric between my fingers but felt its soft worn squares on my entire body as I remembered Morris lowering me onto this quilt that never kept straw from poking into my back.

This was my box, filled with objects I had touched so many times I did not need to concentrate to remember why I kept them. For seventeen years I avoided the thought of Morris. It seemed now the memory of him pursued me as intently as Morris had before I agreed to marry him. I remembered snatches of his letters by the V-mail dates.

The headline "Local Boys Answer the Call" reminded me of our fiercest argument. He had driven through the middle of the fields in his truck across the rows of harvested corn. He wanted me to leave the horses in the field and drive with him to the courthouse to marry. I had never needed a license to name who I was to Morris. I could not see leaving corn to harvest with a snowstorm threatening to slow me down. Morris enlisted the following day.

I had forgotten this box filled with his letters and newspaper articles tracking his infantry. I tucked the flaps in on themselves so I could heave the sealed box out the window. I lifted the box over my shoulder but rested it on the window ledge at the sight of my father's belongings scattered across the yard. I could care less if the neighbors thought I was crazy for tossing boxes out the window, but I did not want any of them to mistake Morris as the cause.

I opened my parents' closet and discovered that my father had filled his own closet with boxes before they overflowed into the closet in the spare room. He had "Magazines to Read," "Leaf Collection," and "Bibles to Give Away." Another unlabeled box sat on the closet shelf. I hesitated, assuming it also held reminders of Morris, yet I would never have stored this in my parents' closet. I took down the unlabeled one and sat on the bedroom floor until my legs went numb beneath me.

The box was filled with receipts for horses, a moldboard plow, livestock, and lumber. The receipts documented purchases my father made from merchants in every town from Carson to Ashland. I separated the receipts from loan agreements, trying to make sense of them. The papers had absorbed the smell of cardboard and mothballs. The smudge of carbon paper on the receipts revealed them to be copies, though I doubted that anyone had the originals, as some were dated before my birth. At first, I flipped through the loan documents quickly, scanning for words to make sense of them, then slowed and read every receipt, which all ended the same. My uncle had paid the balance.

At the bottom of the box I found my grandfather's will. The force of the typewriter keys left tracks across the back of the onionskin paper. *In the name of God, Amen. I, Eugene Connell, of the county of Richland and the State of Ohio, being weak in body, but of sound and perfect mind and memory blessed be the Almighty God for the same.*

I knew the will without reading it. I came to a gradual understanding of a story that my father would never tell. As I child I grasped that my grandfather loved one son better than the other, something I knew fathers were capable of. My uncle lost his father's favor by leaving for college, and yet I had not gained my own father's favor by staying.

A small leather-bound book, its rotting cover held together by twine, revealed that my father had not been the first to wrestle profits from the land. My grandfather had inherited soil that mere crop rotation had not replenished. Folded in this book, a letter from C. G. Hoffman at Farmer's First National noted his friendship with my grandfather as if it were equity or collateral. According to the figures preceding this letter, my grandfather had little else to offer. The letter outlined terms so generous the debt passed to my father fully intact. My father had assumed the debt as if he had caused it, never alluding to it as anything other than his duty. A letter from Farmer's alerted my father to Hoffman's death but said nothing of the loan. A later letter, signed by my Uncle Charlie, addressed the new terms of the loan.

Dear Brother,

The files related to our family farm, as I will always consider it, came across my desk. As you know, our father's friendship with Mr. Hoffman allowed for lenient terms. Farmer's expansion has caused us to revisit these handshake loans made too frequently by Mr. Hoffman. In order to maintain the trust of our customers that we avoid unprofessional favoritism, you will find our standard loan documents enclosed.

The documents were still enclosed with my father's notations in the margins. He had circled the figures with such force that shadow circles were pressed into the next page. I could find no record of who suggested that Charlie assume a loan my father could never pay, though I suspected it had been Charlie's plan from the beginning. The next loan agreement indicated that Charlie had paid the bank and all of the merchants my father owed. I skimmed over these documents, their words holding no meaning. I flipped to the end of the letter where my father had penned his name without the slightest hesitation. The date next to his name revealed far more than the agreement ever would. My father had signed all of them in the weeks following my brother's death. And I understood, as if the thought had always been with me, that my father had not wanted me as his heir.

He had known, as my years of saving had shown, that I would never earn enough to own this land. Though I had promised him that I would farm this land, he had sided with my mother all along.

Chapter Ten

I held tightly to Mattie's hand as we crossed the four lanes at Main Street. Mattie's hand felt small and distant, with our gloves padding us from the awkwardness of walking through the city connected to one another. Mattie could not match my stride but she matched my speed as we nearly jogged across the street. It was colder in the city. The buildings trapped the cold air like a root cellar. Mansfield was gray. Even the spits of snow looked gray before they turned to slush under men's wingtip shoes.

I had never come to town on a Wednesday. I had certainly never come to town on a Wednesday to shop at Reed's. Mattie needed school clothes and not the sort that Morris bought for her. If I enrolled Mattie in school, Rex could hardly ask me to move before June. I needed time to work out a plan.

We walked toward North Park Street past the more affordable department stores. Men walked briskly around us with their heads tucked against the wind. They held their hats with one hand and briefcases with the other. My mother had wanted this for me. She told me of men who left for work dressed smartly in suits and hats and who returned in time for supper. She believed these men read the newspaper and drank coffee with their wives rather than spending their first hours in the barn. I couldn't decide if the joke was on my mother or me that Morris became one of these men.

As we neared Reed's, we passed the Leland Hotel with its doorman who seemed as aloof as the patrons. Reed's large windows displayed Easter dresses with pastel sashes and wide, white collars. A large black sign as tall as the windows advertised in gold embossed letters, "H. L. Reed & Co. The Old Reliable." Pink pinstriped awnings jutted from the display windows overlooking the park with its benches surrounding a band shell that promised warmer seasons.

Entering Reed's, Mattie shook her hand free of mine. She primly removed her hat and gloves in the shaft of warmth. Easter hats paraded across the glass countertop near the door. Feathers from proud birds, ostriches and peacocks, protruded awkwardly from the backs of pink, orange, and lime green hats.

Without glancing over her shoulder to see if I followed, Mattie walked toward the elevator. She pressed the up button while I looked at the store directory to find the children's department. The elevator attendant unlatched the gold-plated accordion gate and slid it to the side. Mattie informed her that we wanted the second floor.

Even if the store dressed me in their finest, as they had this young woman, Reed's would never hire me to operate an elevator. I did not have the figure of a mannequin. But I could not tolerate the idea of any of the jobs available to me in this town, sitting indoors on the assembly line at Ohio Brass or Tappan or sitting at a desk typing dictation.

When we reached the second floor, the elevator operator opened the door. Mattie walked directly to the children's department with her arm cocked at her side as if she held a purse. A saleswoman standing at the edge of the department apparently knew Mattie, and her face contorted to a look more distressed than real grief.

As she tried to tell me how saddened the staff had been at the news, I interrupted her. "We're just looking."

"I'm shopping for a new dress," Mattie told her.

Mattie had not forgotten my promise for a new dress before she went to school. But she refused to pick her dress from a catalogue, which would require another two weeks for delivery. I planned to take her to Montgomery Ward or J. C. Penney's, but then she said her mother always shopped at Reed's. An extra five dollars wouldn't help me bargain with Rex, so I took money saved for seed.

The credenzas of clothes wearied me as Mattie turned them by tugging on the hems of the dresses. Music strained from the speakers overhead with a melody too simple to draw attention to itself, if one forgot to listen.

The saleswoman stepped in front of me and politely asked what dresses Mattie wanted to try on. As Mattie pointed to dresses, the saleswoman draped them over her arm and took them into a dressing room. I flipped over the tag of the nearest dress. Nineteen dollars. We could not afford to shop here. Mattie ignored my motion to leave before the saleswoman returned.

I sat in the chair closest to the dressing room as I waited for Mattie. Pleated pink pillows with large buttons made it difficult to settle back in the chair. I unzipped my coat but didn't remove it. The saleswoman might think we planned to buy these dresses if I appeared too comfortable.

Mattie modeled each dress, walking slowly from the dressing room and then turning in a full circle as if by command. For a moment I saw how Zela had spent her time and money. The saleswoman watched my reaction as Mattie sashayed to and from the dressing room. Before I could stop the saleswoman, she had gathered another armful of dresses for Mattie and taken them into the dressing room.

"You can't say no to this one," Mattie shouted from behind the pink curtain. Mattie held herself stiffly as she stood in front of me. This dress had none of the lace or ribbons of the others. It was a sensible plaid jumper with a solid navy turtleneck underneath. This was the first outfit she could wear in the lingering days of winter.

The saleswoman handed me a pair of matching navy tights and said, "These will keep her legs warm. Shall I find more dresses in this style?"

I nodded so that the woman would leave us. I whispered to Mattie, "Let's go to Penney's."

"Why?"

"They'll have the same jumper for half the price."

"You don't know how much it is."

I glanced at the chandelier in the women's department behind us and ran my hand over the plush fabric of the chair. "It's too expensive."

"You promised," she said.

"Not from Reed's. I never said I would buy the dress here."

"I don't want to go to your school. I have my own school," Mattie said raising her voice.

"Put your clothes back on." I stood and zipped up my coat. "And don't come out until you can act sensibly."

The saleswoman had intercepted another customer near the display of nineteen-dollar Easter dresses. This woman clearly had the means to purchase these dresses. In fact she wore the same outfit as the mannequin we passed in the women's department. Had she worn an apron over the white blouse, yellow cardigan, and matching yellow skirt, she could have stepped into an advertisement for dish soap. The saleswoman would forget us as long as this woman was in her department.

Then the saleswoman pointed toward us, and I knew before her customer turned toward me that she was Morris's wife. I wanted to join Mattie in the dressing room and draw the curtain shut until Charlotte left the store, but I was stunned by her nearness. After they first married, I sat in my truck outside Morris's house watching this woman illumined by the light above the kitchen table as she arranged flowers in a vase, set the silverware, carried the dishes to the table.

Now as she walked toward me, I studied her for a glimpse of myself. A smile. A shrug. A smirk. I looked for anything that might reveal how Morris's attraction for me caused him a moment of misplaced longing for her. But I saw nothing of myself in her tapered calves that narrowed into ankles precariously supported by high heels. The hand she extended to shake was warmed from an afternoon of shopping and softened by cream that left the smell of sugared peaches on my hand.

She was perfectly drawn. She had outlined her eyes in black circles and lined her lips with red. Her trim blouse was tucked into a pleated skirt with ironed creases. I could not see her naked in the crook of Morris's arm eased back into hay bales with only a quilt to keep her warm. I could not imagine him picking bits of hay from her hair or carrying her quietly into a moonlit pond where they would sink to their ankles in mud. She seemed too proper for Morris's passion.

"Aunt Charlotte," Mattie yelled through the dressing room curtain as Charlotte introduced herself. Mattie brought out the jumper and an impractical yellow dress embroidered with daisies. "I'll wear one to school and the other to church." She handed them to me confidently as if challenging me to refuse her in front of Charlotte. Without looking at the price tags, I patted my coat for the checkbook I carried in my pocket. A chill ran through me as I realized that secrets weren't easily hidden from children.

I milked alone that afternoon. Stanley had borrowed the truck for errands as soon as we returned from Mansfield. Mattie washed her hair for school the next day because I wanted it dry enough for rollers that night. The small smile that had played on Mattie's lips after I bought the dresses spread into a full grin when she realized she would bathe rather than milk. She unwrapped the lavender soap, another gift from Charlotte, that she kept in a tissue under the sink for her Saturday night baths. I did not want to consider the cost of Mattie's happiness. I simply wanted to spend the afternoon alone.

It seemed foolish that after seventeen years I could not accept that Morris loved Charlotte. This wave of longing would pass. I would finish the milking, and by the time I walked back to the house I would stop wondering why.

The cow's crooked-jaw chewing comforted me with the quiet munching of hay. Resting my head on her bristly side, I breathed in the familiar stench of flesh and feed and feces. I blinked harshly and tugged on the teats with force. After all I had given, I could not allow myself to consider that I could lose this farm.

I did not turn when the door creaked open. I waited for Stanley to turn on the water to scrub out a bucket to join me. Instead Morris pulled a straw bale next to me, which, when he sat, placed him slightly higher than me on my milking stool. He nodded and I nodded back. He leaned forward, propping his elbows on his knees, twirling a charcoal felt suit hat between his hands. Had he not worn a gray suit with a light blue shirt, he could have been his father.

"Have you really been gone long enough to forget?" I asked. "Never thought a Brubaker would interrupt milking."

"Who says I didn't come to help?"

"If I thought you remembered how, I'd let you."

Morris grinned and took off his suit jacket and rolled up his sleeves. "Is that so?"

"I'll give you a head start." I handed him my bucket and reached behind me for another one that I had disinfected. I patted the cow in front of him. "This is a cow."

Morris laughed, and I relaxed into the rhythm of filling the bucket in front of me. At first he moved his hands awkwardly, but within moments our steady squirts of milk filled the silence. The blond hair on his arms had thickened, yet the muscles that tensed as he worked the milk from the teats reminded me of the hours we had worked side by side.

I felt young with Morris beside me. My body relaxed as if I had been outside too long and now I stood near a fire. Until he left for the war, I had not known an afternoon after my brother's death without working beside him. Facing these cows we had admitted our doubt in the hymn sung at my brother's funeral. God's faithfulness did not seem great and my brother's death felt hidden in the darkest shadow of God's turning from us. It was right to have Morris beside me again.

"I doubt you drove all this way for milking," I said, as I wiped my hands and set my bucket to the side. "Though I'm tempted to hire you. Brubakers always had a way with farming."

"God rest my great-grandfather's soul. A woman offering to hire his kin to work in his valley." Morris made the sign of the cross. A motion so foreign it seemed he had taken several steps away from me. I heard rumors of Charlotte's Catholicism but not of Morris's conversion. A short pain coursed through me. More than marking him as a Catholic, it marked him as hers, a fact I had forgotten for nearly twenty minutes.

"I said tempted. I wouldn't actually hire you."

"Why not?"

"I can't have my workers leaving without explanation," I said, regretting my words as soon as I spoke. We had been enjoying one another and I didn't want that to change.

"Fair enough," he said. Morris unrolled his sleeves and buttoned them. I turned my stool toward him.

"I suppose you brought another shopping bag of dresses that Mattie can't wear." When he raised his eyebrows in a question, I answered, "I saw Charlotte at Reed's today in the children's section."

"Mattie told her she's starting school tomorrow."

"That's right. I've put it off too long."

"I've tried to give you space to make a decision, Dottie. I hoped to talk this through before you sent her off to a . . . ," Morris hesitated, "school." I wondered what derogatory adjective he had skipped over.

"What do we need to talk over?"

"We live minutes from her school. At least let her finish off the year with a familiar teacher and class."

"And then you'll suggest that I let her spend the summer swimming at a familiar country club, and then come fall you'll want her back in a familiar school."

"What's wrong with that?"

"It's not what Zela wanted. Zela wanted her to be familiar with this valley," I said, though part of me wanted to yield to him. She could spend her Saturdays shopping at Reed's as she had with Zela, and she would be raised by a Brubaker.

Morris moved closer to me. So close I could smell the soft scent of his aftershave and taste a feeling as palpable as spring air and the remembrance of warmth. "You've changed, Dottie. You should smile. You're beautiful when you smile."

"And you're transparent when you flatter." I checked myself from ending with a smile. Though in his way, he had almost drawn it from me.

"I need to be honest with you," he whispered. "Charlotte cannot have children." For a moment a slight thrill ran through me at the thought that Charlotte could be flawed. I ached to reach out to him to comfort him. As he leaned toward me, I felt the warmth of him moving on me in this barn. I felt the old fear mixed with the hope that my father would find us so that we would have no choice but to marry immediately. I wanted to tell him that we would have had sons. Brubakers to carry on the family name.

"I'm sorry," I said.

"It has been the greatest pain of my life not to share the joy of children with my wife," he said. He pinched the top of his nose as he had when we said good-bye, as he always had when tears threatened to fall. "I've never wanted anything more."

I was a fool. I stood briskly, nearly knocking over the bucket near me. I touched the back of my hand to my cheek.

"Sometimes you have to live with pain." I picked up my stool and hung it on the pegs behind me. "Your sister entrusted me with Mattie," I said, though my loyalty to Zela did not account for the sudden stubbornness to keep Mattie from him. "I'm keeping her."

"For spite or money?" Morris's cheek flinched as he worked for composure. "A yellow-page lawyer," he said, as he studied my face. "You set it up, didn't you? You told Zela to call my secretary for the will and helped her find another lawyer."

"I did no such thing." My look was as severe as my words.

"She never had a head for business. You found a lawyer you could deal with later."

I assumed that I had outgrown wanting this sort of argument with Morris. "You're jealous that your sister didn't trust you with her child." The words tasted right in my mouth. I wanted to hurt him, and then I understood that all the arguments I had imagined having with Morris and practiced having with Morris still existed. I used different words with old emotions.

Lost in our sudden burst of shouting was the truth. I had never visited Zela's lawyer. Morris grabbed his coat. "I never thought you this low, Dottie, to take a child for money." Morris pulled on his gloves. As he brushed past me, he whispered, "Try thinking of someone other than yourself."

Chapter Eleven

Mothers gathered near the coat rack at the Presbyterian church like squirrels around a corncob in winter. They chatted with the ones closest to them and looked around often to wave or call out greetings to others gathered throughout the foyer. The burst of heat overhead stirred up the smell of other homes. The mothers took off their children's coats, straightened dresses and ties, and told the children not to run through God's house.

I watched these mothers. I had decided that mothering could be studied, and I intended to learn. In the month that Mattie had spent with me, I had not considered that I would become her mother, yet within moments I had backed myself into fighting for a child I had not intended to keep.

The mothers changed into high-heeled shoes near the coat rack. Their boots were lined up nearby, shedding chunks of gray slush from the parking lot. I wiped the soles of my boots on the gray mat inside the foyer. I had not thought to bring shoes to change into, and my stocking feet were sweating already.

I helped Mattie take off her coat, though I thought her old enough to do it on her own. Mattie kicked her boots off under the coats and waved to me to hand her her coat. From her coat pocket, she took out her shoes. She looked at my boots.

"My feet get cold," I said.

I joined the mothers hanging their families' coats together. More mothers entered the church and were hugged by the ones already crowded together. I hung our coats quickly.

I guided Mattie away from the crowd, afraid someone would notice that we were newcomers and say something polite. There were few people I recognized. These were city people who had come to Carson to live in houses crowded on small lawns at the edge of town. The residents were young and Presbyterian, so I had little chance of knowing them. Mattie had declared herself a Presbyterian on the way to Carson, which suited me. I'd grown up with the Methodists' version of God, whom I'd never been able to please.

Mattie and I were the first in the sanctuary. The pews had no pew cushions. The oak back curved into the seat. By concentrating on sitting straight on the highly polished pews, I managed to stop feeling as if I would slide to the floor.

In the Methodist church, we had sat on cracked, donated theater seats that folded up when we stood to sing hymns. My family sat in seats thirty through thirty-three every Sunday until the church collected enough money to purchase pews.

The Presbyterians had large paneled lights hung on thick chains from the high ceiling. A skinny gold cross marked the middle of each panel. The room was warm. I rubbed my neck with my handkerchief and then remembered I should dab, which I did, though it took longer. The mothers and fathers rejoined one another and proceeded into the church with their children between them.

The organ pipes at the front of the church groaned with loud, quick chords. Mattie held out the hymnal. As I sang, I saw two torn pieces of paper sticking out from other parts of the hymnal, marking the next hymns. Mattie was prepared.

A person behind me tapped the toe of his boot to the four-count rhythm as he sang, "The sea waves cold, threaten the soul." I recognized his voice. When we ended the song, Mattie flipped to the second hymn, and I turned slightly to look behind me. Rex nodded hello. He wore a checkered shirt and a brown braided leather bolo tie with an oval agate stone. I had not heard from him in a few days and had secretly hoped he had flown back to California for warmth. I suspected that he would raise his hand when they asked if there were newcomers. He did, and I did not.

I opened the Bible when the mother beside me opened hers. Mattie found the passage in the book of Mark before I could hand it to her. After the Scripture reading, they told the children to go to children's church. She seemed to expect this, and she followed the other children out toward the foyer.

"Why are you afraid?" the pastor began. His voice reminded me of the first grumble of a tractor engine before it turned over. I read ahead. A storm had heaved enough water into the boat that carried Jesus and His disciples that the disciples believed they would drown. Jesus slept in the midst of it. This, the pastor said, should bring us great peace. He called the disciples faithless. I read the passage again. The storm ended only after the disciples woke Jesus, but the pastor spoke only of Jesus calming the storm. It seemed if they had simply waited for God to save them, their ship would have sunk in the storm.

With Rex behind me, it was difficult to consider the sermon. Even though my father had made no effort to save the farm for me, I would not sit back and wait for Rex to take it from me. I knew as I stood to sing the final hymn that I would not leave this church without a promise from Rex to leave town.

Rex waited for me at the end of my pew as the congregation filed out. "I drove downtown thinking I should meet the church crowd," Rex said, as he shuffled his hat between his hands. "When I saw your truck, I thought you could introduce me to the people that mattered."

"Then let me introduce myself." I shook his hand. "I'm Dottie Connell."

He smiled. "Really, Dottie."

Mothers followed their children, reshelved pew hymnals, and collected boys' suit jackets as they made their way to the foyer. I lowered my voice. "How much do you want for the farm?"

"At church?" Rex whispered. "Do you have more money than you offered last week?"

"I may," I said, admitting to myself for the first time that I would be willing to visit the lawyer to find out how much money Zela had left Mattie and if I could borrow against it.

"I can't make a deal with money you may have."

"I have an inheritance."

"From who?"

"That's neither here nor there. What matters is that your father has two afflictions, his age and his money, and neither can secure what he wants."

Rex smiled. "If you believe you understand my father, you've accomplished something I haven't."

"I know he's wealthy and my money means nothing to him, or else I'd buy the farm directly from him. But you're young, Rex. You should sell the farm before you learn there won't be any profit."

"I'm suspicious of your business tactics, Dottie. You curse the farm to me and fight for it for yourself."

The church door opened, echoing loudly when it shut. Mattie stood on the other side. She had found her coat and wore her boots. She waved. I motioned for her to wait.

"If you don't make me an offer, Rex, I'll lose my nerve," I said. I returned the Bible to the wooden rack on the back of the pew and took the torn paper bookmarks from Mattie's hymnal.

"Three hundred," he said. I tilted my head, confused. "Three hundred thousand," he clarified.

I folded my arms and slowly shook my head. I could not imagine that Mattie's inheritance would be enough. "It's the price of two farms."

Mattie, impatient to leave, came into the pew and tugged on my dress. "Look what they gave me for being new." She showed me a bookmark. "I told them we would come back."

My words came out stiff and awkward. "Be a good girl and see if my coat is still hanging up." She ran down the aisle. Her coat flared behind her. I sighed.

I turned to Rex and said to him, to myself, "It's not worth that."

"That's my price," he said.

Chapter Twelve

If I was a young woman, I might have worn perfume and red lipstick to the lawyer's office. If I was a beautiful woman, I might have worn a black dress that slid down my body. But I was neither, so I dressed warmly for the drive to Mansfield and took all of the money I had from the safe in my office, wondering if the lawyer had ever accepted a bribe before and if so, if mine would seem pitiful by comparison.

Zela's yellow-page lawyer had the largest advertisement in the phone book and the smallest office on the fourth floor of an office building on Park Avenue West. The empty waiting room had four brown vinyl chairs lined against the wall. A philodendron drooped in the corner.

I cleared my throat and heard the rustling of paper in the office, but no one came out. Peeking through the slightly opened door, I saw a plump man with a pile of paper balls that he methodically picked up and shot toward a trash can. I backed away from the door and said hello. He yelled that he would be with me in a minute. When he invited me into his office, he had cleared the desk of paper balls.

He mopped his face with a handkerchief and asked if I had an appointment. After pointing to the seat that I should sit in, he told me I was fortunate to catch him on a day where his calendar wasn't full with clients. He leaned back in his chair and spread his stubby fingers across his stomach and asked why I had come. Even his tiny earlobes puffed past their capacity. Before I could answer, he said he should get us both some coffee. He yelled for his secretary, who did not materialize.

"Please excuse me. I'll see if she can get us coffee."

His diploma, the solitary wall hanging, confirmed why Zela had come here. He had no plaques of appreciation from the United Way or marbled trophies from golf tournaments. Though Zela could have afforded any lawyer in town, she had apparently found one with whom her husband and brother would not have associated.

Her meticulous planning unsettled me. I could no longer assure myself that she set her house ablaze in a moment of anger. Her quiet walks alone on my farm were not simply a desire for solitude. Her preparation had required time and silence. I should have gone to her in the fall when she sat for hours on the rubber tire swing tied to the old oak, staring toward the farm that had been her family's.

The lawyer returned with steaming cups of coffee in each hand.

"She must have stepped out. It's hard to keep good help these days."

The office smelled of damp file folders and dust that settled in my throat. I thanked him for the coffee.

He remembered Zela. Stylish. Nice. Intelligent. He smiled as he talked of her. He also remembered my name. As he rummaged through files stacked on top of the file cabinet, he said, "I've tried calling you many times. You didn't come when I read the will. No one has heard the entire will read. Her brother got in such a huff when I mentioned the little girl that he stormed out of my office."

I murmured empathetically. I smiled and laughed too loudly when he described his frustration of sitting in an empty room with the will.

Water spots spread like coffee stains across the ceiling. "Times hard, Mr. Johnson?"

He leaned back in his chair, pushing back his shoulders, smiling with pride. "I work for myself and set my own hours."

"I know that life. It doesn't guarantee a paycheck."

He leaned forward in his chair. "Remind me, ma'am. How can I help you this fine morning?"

Since Sunday, I had worked my words over in my mind. I had been so confident of my success that I told Rex to meet me at the courthouse at noon. Regardless of the amount of the inheritance, I could negotiate with Rex at the courthouse if I held cash in my hand. We would walk directly to the title department before he had time to change his mind or talk to his father.

"What sort of . . ." I paused. I had gotten myself out of order. Heat flushed my body. I fanned myself, but the heat hovered over every inch of my skin.

"What I was wondering, sir, is the amount of Mattie's inheritance?"

"Didn't your uncle tell you?" He mopped his face again. "Normally I wouldn't have done this, but he assured me he managed your financial affairs. It seemed like a small town approach to me, but he showed me the deed for the farm you ran."

Before he could say more I raised my hand. His prattling only infuriated me more and revealed he had known better. Had I not needed the money, I would have screamed at the man for his incompetence and threatened to close his pitiful office, but instead I said sweetly, "You'll have to remind me what you told him."

He opened another drawer of his desk and looked through the files. "It's substantial." He pulled out the file and propped reading glasses on his nose. "It's three hundred thousand dollars."

"Of course," I said, trying to remain calm though I couldn't take in what Charlie had done. I ran my hand over the ripped leather arm of the chair. The heat from the radiator was sickening, and the dull greens of the office only hastened the feeling that I would need to run for the trash can. The lawyer went on about phone calls and how I had not called him. Hatred was a futile emotion with my uncle. One must remain calm to win.

Of course Charlie would have thought to make phone calls after seeing notice of the fire in the newspaper. Nathaniel's success was well-known, and Charlie would recognize how much money that type of achievement was worth. Before I had known if I would raise Mattie, Charlie had called his son home. So this was what his son's affection cost him?

Rex would not sign over the title without the amount his father promised him, and even if Rex did not want my farm, my uncle would never go back on his threat to take it from me. He would take my home. Where would I raise Mattie?

"What sort of fee is required to withdraw Mattie's inheritance?"

He scrunched his eyebrows together and asked, "Fee?" as though he had never heard the word.

"What would you charge," I tried again, "I'm sure there must be some. . . ." Words failed me. "Some arrangement to get the money." I thought from the look of his office I would have an easier time of it.

He talked again of trying to call me, and I slumped back in my chair. In only thirty minutes I would meet Rex, and even though I knew their plan, it wouldn't end until I handed Rex the money. I interrupted him again. "Would you withdraw it for five hundred dollars?"

"I can't withdraw the money," he said.

"I need the money today," I interrupted, then smiled and tried to pace my words. "Surely, you could find a way to withdraw it."

"That's why I tried to call you. I have the savings booklet here. Zela had me keep it here with the will."

"Why did she do that?" I asked. My satin blouse clung to my back. The heater clanked and roared with hot air from the coiled register.

"She explained it in the will. Would you like me to read it to you?"

I shook my head and sat forward in my seat. "Tell me what it says in plain talk."

"She trusted you to spend the money to raise the little girl. Once she turns eighteen, you must give her the remaining money. The money is in an account at the

Richland Bank." He handed me the passport-size savings book. The number of the account had been written in Zela's perfect handwriting. The figure in the right column matched the amount the lawyer had said.

"What do I owe you?" I asked quietly.

He waved me away. "Zela took care of everything. She paid me generously in advance."

I took one hundred dollars from my purse and set it on his desk. "I'd appreciate if neither of us ever talk of this meeting." I tucked the savings book in my purse, shook his hand, and walked outside. The cold was a relief.

I walked three blocks to the bank, keeping my head down against the wind. I bumped into a woman who apologized for stepping in my way. "Sorry," she said. The word was easier between strangers.

The warmth of the bank made my eyes water. I stood in line, mopping my nose, wanting to look assured so that I could feel assured. I wished the lawyer had taken my five hundred dollars. Bribing him would have been easier than learning that Zela trusted me with the money.

"Next," the bank teller called.

The bank would give me a check, not cash. To type the check she wanted to know the recipient.

"Rex," I said.

The chain on the teller's glasses shook as she chomped her gum. "Got it. Last name?"

"Once you type the check, that's it? I can't get it back?"

She stared at me as though my question was too basic to answer. She nodded. "That's what you said. Cashier's check for three hundred." She turned the savings book around and showed me. "That closes the account. Do you want to step aside, ma'am, and think this over? There's a line of people."

Rex waited at the courthouse where they would type my name at the top of a title. Charlie would never come for another rent payment. If I handed this check to Rex, the title of ownership would be in my name, and Mattie could grow up where Zela had intended.

"Connell," I said. "His last name is Connell."

Few stores stood near the bank, only a wig shop, a woman's dress shop, and a camera shop. A small bell alerted the camera store clerk when I came in the door. No one had washed the spray-painted Christmas snow from the door. Rows of cameras lined shelves behind a glass case, which held even more expensive cameras. I studied the full round face of a camera as the clerk rapidly explained it. "Two or three aperture settings, single-speed shutter, 'pin and screw' flash with twelve exposures, and an ever-ready case." He sold me the Brownie 44a with a package of 127-speed film for thirty-five dollars. At the drug store near the parking meter, I would buy lavender-flowered wrapping paper and leave the wrapped gift for Mattie to find on the kitchen table after her evening chores.

Part Two

1972

Chapter Thirteen

Working against the fading daylight, I forked straw between the rows of blackberry vines but looked for Mattie, who had abandoned her work in the garden. Straw bales tossed from the back of my '67 Ford sat at the four corners of the berry patch. I shook the fork like a flour sifter, scattering the straw to keep the soil moist. I would pick two hundred quarts of blackberries before the summer's end and an equal quantity of blueberries if I could ward off the robins.

Mansfielders had reacted to an unnatural war by buying what they called natural food. My profits in berries had surpassed my failed hog venture, by which I had meant to regain a portion of Mattie's inheritance but instead created more debt.

I preferred buying the piglets, which smelled like hickory nuts. The hogs had sense uncommon to most creatures and an admirable desire to escape. Even the electric fence did not deter them; instead, they squealed as they ran toward it, anticipating the shock. I enjoyed chasing down a loose hog, as opposed to chasing the berry buyers from my porch. The berry buyers called my land paradise, as though what they saw was a result of rocking on the porch.

The sun rested in its fireside light, flickering shadows across the valley. A westward shadow gave the look of two hoes propped in the kitchen garden. Mattie had quit in the middle of the pea plants while I worked backward through the berry patch. Mattie hated peas. When I had given her the paper sack full of Burpee seed packages for her garden, she sorted through the packets and handed back the peas. The vegetables agreeable to her were tomatoes, green peppers, and yellow squash, conspicuous vegetables that required little stooping and no work once she picked them. She resisted growing anything in the garden that had to be shelled, snapped, or husked. She informed me that they sold peas in the grocery store, shelled, frozen, and ready to eat. I made her plant an extra row for believing that food came easily.

She said she could not please me, but she did. When angered, she could hoe the garden in a mere forty minutes. From my vantage point at other chores, I would occasionally stop at the sight of a woman working fast in the garden. I saw our future and was pleased. With her dark hair twisted in a braid and covered with a bandanna and her hands protected by yellow cowhide gloves, I saw how time would reverse our positions and take her to the fields and leave me to care for things closer to the house. I waited for the right time to tell her I was proud of her, when I would also tell her that the farm was hers. A right time would come.

I stabbed the pitchfork in a mound of straw and went in search of her. The time had come to speak of other matters. Thinking of it as "other matters" made me worry that I could not raise the subject with Mattie. Prudery did not account for my euphemisms, but lack of conversations did. My mother had laid a book on my pillow the night of my seventeenth birthday, *A Young Lady's Private Counselor.* Zela spoke of *it* once, when she promised shortly after her marriage that if I were to marry she would tell me what the *Lady's Private Counselor* would not. Morris and I had never needed a book.

Talking as we worked was a more natural way to chat with Mattie. So a few days after Mattie suggested it, I picked out a box of hair coloring, even though Stanley had shaken his head at the mention of it. He said he liked the silver strands of moonlight in my hair.

On the path near the wooded field, Mattie lay on her belly. She held her camera steady by propping herself up on her elbows. I stopped far enough away that the wild turkey she focused on would not take for the woods. Any other photographer would have put the sunset in the background, but Mattie did not have an eye for these things. I saw her photographs every Monday when I dropped off new rolls and picked up developed ones at the Shutter Bug. I allowed three rolls a week in exchange for her chores. The hobby entertained both of us.

If Banjo had survived being clipped by a car, he would have chased the turkey from the path. Mattie rolled onto her back. Corn kernels she had scattered on the path preoccupied the turkey. An entire roll would be wasted on this bird. The previous week, she had taken a whole roll's worth of barn kittens and had not gotten one single kitten in a pose. Her pictures were not cuddly calendar poses. The pincushion bottom of a paw. A scaly, watery nose. A fan of whiskers cutting through a shaft of barn light.

Whenever she took the camera to school, I examined the pictures. This was the reason I went to the Shutter Bug each week, to scan the pictures for young men in her class. Fortunately they only intruded with rabbit ears, mouths stretched to ovals, and white eyeballs.

Mattie occasionally appeared in these photographs with two friends, Trudy and Pauline. Mattie was the leader of the trio that formed in the Sunday school room at the Presbyterian church. Their friendship survived the move from Maplewood Elementary to the larger, newly constructed Carson High School.

They attempted womanhood, at least the magazine variety, in glossy three-by-three inch squares. They toyed with beaded necklaces and shared a pair of thin-wired granny glasses that I'd seen in the pictures of John Lennon that were taped to Mattie's wall. The girls posed in knee-high white boots that appeared, in turn, on all of them. Pauline's older sister had donated the outdated fashions.

Regardless of how Trudy posed, her nose looked pinched and solemn. Pauline already had her mother's hefty figure. They always looked ready to giggle the moment Mattie took the picture. Mattie was brave for the camera. She was beautiful.

Crawling after the wild turkey, she was a prettier, bolder version of her mother. The bird fluttered and pecked at the trail she'd intended for it. She slipped around it and came up on the other side. Had she been a hunter her mark would be easy, her turkey bagged and brought down for dinner by the time she decided on her next picture. Her dark hair was lost in the wood's shadow where she hid. Then she saw me and lowered the camera. She thrashed through the deadwood and brush at the edge of the woods. The bird squawked and wobbled down the path. She fastened the case over the camera and slung the strap over her shoulder.

"I forgot the peas," she said, as she walked toward me. The sun had lowered behind the valley hills and left only a gray light. Fireflies appeared, as the moon did, as if they had been there all along. "I'll put the floodlight on and hoe them tonight."

"And hoe up every pea plant along with them?" She did not see my smile. She had already started down the path. It took two steps to match her stride. "They can wait until morning."

She stopped. "You didn't come about the peas?"

"I've got a box of Lady Clairol and a few hours to spare." I took off my baseball cap and snapped it to my belt. I fluffed my hair that had grown to my shoulders.

"And cover your moonlit streaks?" she asked in the playful rolling way of Stanley's voice.

By the light over the kitchen table, Mattie studied the color on the box. The moonlit streaks would remain, at least until I made another trip to Carson. Pauline's hair had turned the color of turnips when they tried this brand. She didn't see why I had chosen auburn. It had too much red.

"Buy this as if it's work gloves or seed," she said, handing back the bottle. "You can't go cheap on this."

I wrapped the folded instructions around the bottle and packed it in the box. "We might as well spend the evening together. I've set the time aside," I said.

In Mattie's hesitation, I understood my mother had been wiser in her mothering. She had never given me the chance to tell her no. Mattie waved for me to follow her and told me she had planned on trying a new nail polish from Charlotte.

"Polish wouldn't last an hour on my hands," I said as I followed her to her room.

"Put it on your toes."

We sat on Mattie's bedroom floor. Wads of toilet paper separated my toes, and I brushed Ice Pink over my nails which were as tough as a turtle shell. Mattie glanced at them. "It's not your color."

I stopped and sunk the brush back into the bottle. She took out a deep brownish-red, the color of boots straight from the box. She handed me a cotton ball thick with the smell of polish remover.

"Some night we should do makeovers. I'd love to see Stanley's face if you got dressed up."

"For what reason?"

"To remind you that you're pretty."

I rubbed my toenails with the cotton ball. "Nothing good comes from a man finding you pretty." I flushed at the memory of Morris swimming under the pond water finding my toes. It had been shameful what that boy could make me feel in the seconds of holding his breath. Given an hour, he made me believe everything about me was beautiful.

"Your mother had good sense with men," I said. Though I doubted the truth of this, Mattie listened when

I mentioned her mother. "She wouldn't kiss your father until they were engaged." I had never believed Zela's courtship of polite words and Sunday visits on her parents' porch to be love. I had doubted it more when the police chief told me the fire started in the bedroom. The newspaper had printed another story blaming faulty wiring in the attic. The printed story became the story everyone assumed to be true, and Mattie had never been told otherwise. I wondered for a moment if I would ever tell her.

"I never saw them kiss," Mattie said, concentrating on perfect lines painted on her toes. I rubbed the cotton ball on my big toe even though I had removed the Ice Pink polish. In ten years, Mattie and I had never talked about her mother's marriage. I feared if I spoke a word she would remember this.

"I don't remember them laughing together," she said. "At least not the way they did when they were apart, the way Dad laughed when we visited Miss Adams." She hesitated. When I did not look up, she continued. "We played cards with Miss Adams, one of Dad's patients. When we went to the park, she would give me malt candies that I wouldn't eat. She and my dad would take walks in the park, and I would wait on the swing set, holding the candies until they melted and made my palms sticky. My mom asked me what made my palms sticky, but my dad had told me not to talk about it. I only told her once, but when I came home with sticky hands she knew where we had been. Did she tell you this about my father?"

"I never knew anyone as loyal as your mother. She would have never said anything against him."

"Did he love my mother when he married her?"

"He thought she was beautiful," I said, because I knew this was true.

"But nothing good comes from that," she said. The deep thrum of the bullfrogs rose around the pond and the shrill reply of the tree frogs cluttered the room with noise. I waited expectantly, hoping Mattie might say more that could help me understand my friend, whom I had loved, whose death I never understood. We painted our nails in silence, hushed by the thought of Zela, until Mattie asked, "Have you ever kissed anyone?"

"What matters is how you let a boy kiss you." I closed the nail polish bottle securely. Then I told her the book's words, wondering if I did little better than my mother when she left the book on my pillow. I said she should stop a boy before he ever kissed her lips. But it was more dangerous if he kissed her neck. Lying next to him, even to talk, could stir desires that would never leave her. If he touched her breast, she had sinned and allowed him to go too far. I told Mattie I knew this from the *Private Counselor's* chapter "The Beginning of Error." The chapter on "Perfect Continence" had the cure. Hard work. If stacking your own woodpile did not dispel your desire, ask a neighbor to help stack his. They recommended fasting and cold baths, though I said nothing of these to Mattie. They had never helped.

"Hard work," I said again, repeating the book's words. "An idle mind will cause you to sin."

Mattie lined the nail polish bottles back in the empty tissue box with the cut-off top. "Can I date now?"

"Not alone," I said.

She flopped her head back and sighed. "So I listened for no reason."

I plucked the toilet paper from between my toes and stood. "You listened to what your mother would have wanted you to hear."

I went to the porch agitated. The wind teased the sweat on the back of my neck. My body had once felt womanly in Morris's arms. My breasts rounded as he pressed me closer to him. I desired, even in the midst of work, to feel my hips shaped by a man's hands.

That first long-ago night, I had felt as if I were the earth filled with the water that fed every stream. The water had rushed behind my ears. It pulsated, needing an outlet. His eyes had the haze of afternoon fields in the sun's heat. He murmured like wind moving over the shadows within the depths of the earth. The breath upon earth created my flesh, and my flesh took on the shape of a woman under his hands. I had never known a sweeter regret.

Chapter Fourteen

June was barren. My basement shelves, long stocked with Mason jars full of dill pickles, green beans, beets, potatoes, peas, and apples, were empty. Only in shadowy corners could I find occasional jars of bread and butter pickles or stewed tomatoes. In the barn, a rock weighed down a pile of empty Pioneer Fielder's Choice seed corn bags. We had planted forty bags, with 80,000 kernels a bag, on one hundred acres. Stanley and I had filled the plastic hoppers with seed and alternated driving the tractor-pulled planter through the fields. Seventy-five acres sprouted the starts of soybeans. My grain bins were oversized birdhouses. The flutter of swallows echoed in the metal bins like sheets left on the line during a windstorm. I smelled harvest in the dust of dried corn that covered the walls of the bins. I would feel unsettled until they were full.

Summer hid death better than any other season. From my porch, the fields appeared green: Granny Smith apple green when wind twisted the leaves with the coming rain, John Deere green with sunrise, and pine needle green under the haze of afternoon heat. I walked the fields often because green, upon close inspection, hid insects and disease. My brother taught me these things when I ran barefoot on the path beside him, begging him to teach me everything he knew. I thought then that his chores would become mine, and I wanted to do them well. I believed that I scrubbed clothes, hung wash, and baked three days a week with my mother only because I was young. When she forced me to iron the same pillow case four times with the flatiron, I only sighed, because I believed I wouldn't need these skills once I was old enough to work with my father and brother. My brother died in the summer. I later learned this was the only reason I took over his chores the following day.

On a Wednesday evening during the first week of June, the rain of the past two weeks stopped and Mattie announced she had a summer job. I had not expected either event. The forecast had called for rain until Friday.

I rubbed Worcestershire sauce on the roast planned for the following day's dinner. Meals followed a scheduled rotation, which I thumbtacked to a pegboard inside the cupboard. I kept fifteen meals on the rotation and cooked the dinner meal before supper each night.

Mattie brought in a quart of strawberries and set them on the counter. She smiled too brightly when she asked if she could help.

"Did you get the quarts ready to sell tomorrow?"

She had and she had already put them on the stand that Stanley had built near the road, so customers could drive by to pick them up. We kept a Hills Brothers can with a slit in the lid for the payments. Trust made some customers so nervous that they parked their cars and searched us out to hand us the cash.

I motioned toward the carrots. "Peel and slice."

Mattie quickly peeled the knuckled carrots into the trash. She asked questions with a politeness used between strangers. I sliced potatoes and answered warily. We had fought the night before when the neighbor boy asked Mattie to the movies. Our arguments never ended this quickly. The boy worked well enough, but his father lacked any sense for farming. The man grew yellow-leafed corn in crooked rows on a piece of property that had once been respected. I had expected Mattie's silence the day after our fight. As a child she had used silence instinctively, as if she would perfect the technique with age, and she had.

"You should come with me tonight," Mattie said. On Wednesdays, she played Scrabble with Stanley. She had used the polished squares to teach him to read when he lived in the room off the machine shed. First she taught him the letters. Then she showed him all the words that ended with *at*, scrambled up the letters, and told him to line up the letters into a word. Now he spent his evenings reading Zane Grey westerns in the small house that he built at the edge of my property. When given the choice, he always worked the field that stood opposite his front window.

"You know I work on the books tonight," I said.

"And Thursday you write out the bills and Friday you iron. And if God takes you up before Sunday, I'm sure

He'll hear how He interrupted something." Mattie laughed and asked how else she could help with supper.

When I pointed toward the table, she asked, "Knives, spoons, or forks?"

"Spoons and forks," I said. I purposefully contradicted my mother's etiquette by not properly setting the table each night. I allowed ketchup bottles on the table, not seeing the need to wash another dish. We used paper napkins instead of cloth and set out only the silverware that was needed. I would have altered my mother's other traits, but Mattie provoked them. If I wrapped an apron over a calico dress that smelled of wood smoke and tied on a dust cap, I would be my mother with her pursed lips and crossed arms. I also spoke her harsh words, which I thought I had disregarded but now used as my own.

"I have a summer job," Mattie said.

"I know you have," I said. "I hired you."

"A camera shop hired me." She studied me for a response, so I gave none. "A camera shop in Mansfield."

"So you're not working for the money." I opened the refrigerator door with my foot and worked the pot roast into an empty spot.

"The pay is good."

"You'd lose it to gasoline costs. Besides, I can't be without you or the truck all day. You get all the film you ask for and Charlotte can't send enough clothes. What more do you want?"

"I'm moving in with my family for the summer. Uncle Morris lives two blocks from the shop. I start tomorrow."

The closer she got to eighteen, the more I felt as if I held a handful of corn kernels. To catch those that slid through my fingers would mean dropping all of them. I ignored her mention of family.

"You have eaten here, enjoyed the warmth of this house, and rested through the winter. All seasons prepare for the next. You have responsibilities here. You can't leave for the summer and expect to enjoy its benefits later." I saw in her eyes what she would say next. So I spoke instead. "Of course, you could choose not to come back. You could choose a life other than the one your mother wanted for you."

Mattie loosened her grip on the chair beside her and walked to my side. "And when I turn eighteen, and you can't say that, I will leave." Mattie walked past me and out the door. The door banged twice before it caught the latch.

I sank to the chair, shaking. The strength needed to calm and focus my anger was gone. I stood and ladled a bowl of soup and tossed my salad for supper. Everything was louder. I heard every bite, every clink of my spoon against the bowl, the hum of the refrigerator, the hollow tick of the cuckoo clock. Nothing, not even when my mother, father, and brother sat around the table, was as loud as this silence.

I poured a glass of store-bought milk and considered that Mattie could leave me. As seasons of floods carved creek banks that remained during seasons of drought, I could never be the woman I was ten years earlier. Not even if I cooked beets in my stew again, sold the Sylvania television, or got a dial tone instead of Pauline's silly laugh when I picked up the phone. I had seen what Mattie and I could share, and it gave purpose to working the land. I walked onto the porch sipping the tasteless milk.

A coming storm bruised the sky to the north. The storm clouds hid in the darkness, appearing as mere variations of blue in the indigo sky. The hue of the barn intensified as though it were 1872 and the Sherwin-Williams brothers had recently painted it Venetian red. The aluminum lightning rods were my only addition to my great-grandfather's gable-roofed building with a single white cupola. He had believed lightning to be God's will and would not interfere. Some called his a simple faith, but it was not simple enough for me to understand. I put lightning rods on a one-hundred-year old building, the only building on the farm that had stood for three generations.

My great-grandfather built his chicken coop behind the barn. My father later dismantled the building, but he told me what his father had told him: that my great-grandfather would have been pleased that he died while working in that coop and that his son went back to work the afternoon he found him dead. I also knew from my father that my grandfather was the first to farm the side hill, and that my father was the first to clear the bottom field. Rex would have never understood the importance of this, and I gambled Mattie's inheritance on a belief that I could explain it to her. I would tell her how the May apples in our woods told the story of my great-grandmother's journey West, and why a hickory nut tree remained in the middle of our cornfield though every other tree had been uprooted.

The sudden thunder sounded hollow. The sky still cast light on the leaves, though no sun could be seen. The wind swirled the leaves as if raindrops tossed them about. The air was cool and damp. But the sky only pretended to rain. Even the wrinkles of heat lightning across the sky did not bring raindrops.

I knew well the specious ways of nature. At forty-eight, I still bled. A barren womb should wither and cease preparing for a child that I would not have. I had once prayed that a baby would be the consequence of my sin. The night before Morris left for war, as he uncovered the quilt we kept under a bale of straw, I prayed we would have a son from our union, though I knew we could not marry in time to save my reputation. Morris and I had already whispered promises in the barn as we pledged our love first with our bodies and then with an engagement ring. I did not want a child as further promise; my yearning for a child of my own existed outside of my desires for Morris.

The door to the machine shed banged open and shut in the wind. I stepped to the edge of the porch to place myself in the way of the wind.

I had meant to live a different life. After Morris returned from the war married, I meant to sketch out another existence without him. That day on the Cincinnati train station platform, I decided I would carry on and make another life.

Morris had telegraphed Zela the time of his arrival, and I took the first morning Greyhound bus out of Mansfield, planning to surprise him. I waited in the middle of the crowd as the train rode in on a gust of air. Everyone wanted the first glance. We had all lived with a war between us, and we hoped, for a last moment, that those who stepped from the train would not have changed. We wished that we had not changed in their absence. I saw this wish in the way wives rearranged their hair and in the way mothers practiced their smiles before the train arrived.

The soldiers lingered on the top step of the train, scanning the crowds. Women beside me stood on tiptoes but waited behind rows of other women. Morris ran down the steps, never looking into the crowd. He did not expect me. Then he turned and offered his hand to the only woman who got off the train of soldiers. I first noticed her profusion of red curls pinned in a fashionable twist. On her lavender suit, she wore an orchid corsage. The newspaper's wedding announcement later described this lavender wedding suit. I managed to get to the bus station before they did and arrived home in time to milk the cows. I knew then I must set my mind to go on. I would earn enough money to buy the farm. I would love and marry another man. I would raise our children. But in the end I had not accomplished any of this.

Chapter Fifteen

I farmed ugly. Others in the valley called it trash farming. I lacked the time and invitation to join the men to jaw at the café on Saturday mornings and talk myself into farming the way men in the valley always had. A few men pulled off to the side of the road to see what I had done with my land. They waved off my explanation, as if it proved a woman should never be given acres of her own. I had not used my moldboard plow in two years. It sat behind the barn with my grandfather's corn drill, a single-horse machine with only one planter shoe.

I imagined that if my mother had seen the unplowed fields, covered with plant residue from two previous harvests, she would have taken her stick broom out and whisked them clean. She loved the look of a horse-plowed field and its neat twelve-inch strips of overturned weeds and broken-up sod. I had loved its smell. The scent of harrowed fields had an affect akin to the smell of sawdust. Hard work wrought that smell.

With trash farming the fields smelled more like corncribs. As Mattie and I walked the fields in the evening, I told her of my mother and her love of a plowed field. I pointed to the hickory nut tree and told her how my grandfather had won first prize for the tastiest hickory nutmeat in Ohio, so the field had been cleared around a single tree. I showed her my girlhood dreaming rock where I would lie, forming plans for my brother and me to work our farm together.

When we walked through the woods, I showed Mattie how my great-grandfather discovered, in the midst of the ferns and the wild columbine, cool water springs that ran deep through the forests. He bought the forested acres, and the spring had never gone dry.

Mattie listened because we had bargained. She walked the farm with me for three evenings to make up work hours spent with Trudy and Pauline at an amusement park, three hours north, built on concreted farm land.

As we walked, I compared my new method of slot tilling to the old moldboard plowing by comparing Mattie's method of dusting furniture to mine. Moldboard plowing followed my method of dusting. I removed from the coffee table the stack of *Farmer's Journal* and *Progressive Farmer*, the macramé coasters, and the ceramic oil lamp. I sprayed the table with Pledge and then dusted in straight lines following the grain of the wood. Mattie left the table as she found it, even if a milk glass from her snack stood in her way. She moved the dust rag between the items. Slot tilling did the same. It opened a slot of land to place the seed and disturbed nothing around it.

Mattie never asked why when I explained these things. I preferred not to tell her that Stanley had first proposed the idea of slot tilling. He had experimented with two small plots for five years and determined it would slow the erosion of topsoil. Only the FHA loan officer knew of Stanley's suggestion, and only because he had refused me a loan for the no-till planter until I told him it was Stanley's idea.

Stanley knocked on the door as I prepared dinner. I added yeast to a bowl of sugar, salt, soda, and buttermilk as he tiptoed into the kitchen. I turned and scowled, a response that brought his laughter.

He went back to the rug to remove his muddy boots. The leather slouched at the ankles. Mud streaked his white socks that had the damp smell of tree roots or mushrooms. "I have never known a woman who love and hate dirt as you do," he said.

"I'd rather sweat over dirt that yields."

Stanley waited on the rug in his sock feet until I asked, "Do you want me to mail you an invitation?"

He came into the kitchen and twirled a kitchen chair on its leg, so he could straddle it and lean forward against the back. I sifted flour into a speckled blue bowl. "The neighbor is cutting hay," he said. Stanley had a smile that twitched as though uncomfortable until it turned to laughter.

"Dad-blast-it, if we haven't had enough rain already. That boy ought to ask us if we want rain before he cuts hay." I grinned. The boy was my age and had, since the age of eleven, rarely cut hay without causing rain.

I sliced lard into the sifted flour. Stanley folded his bandanna to wipe his face. The thermometer read seventy-three degrees, but sweat slid down his forehead. "Dottie, what have I asked for from you?"

I paused from stirring. Stanley had never asked for wages beyond room and board, but I had increased his pay when I learned that he scoffed at talk of Rex coming to farm my land. He told people my cousin was a fast talker who couldn't talk fast enough to fool me. In his ten years of employment, I could only think of two requests, one for himself and the other for Mattie. He asked to drain the swampy land at the edge of the side field as a place to build his two-room cabin, and this summer, he asked that I allow Mattie to work at the camera shop.

"You asked for your house and that I allow Mattie to work in town," I said.

"That makes one yes and one no. So my odds for a yes are fifty-fifty," he said.

I poured the milk mixture over the flour mixture and stirred the dough for the buttermilk rolls. I did not fret over his silence. He obviously had come to ask me a question, and I supposed silence might be easier to answer. I worried that Mattie had put him up to another request.

"Might I borrow the truck?" He twirled his ball cap in his hands.

"Keys are in the ignition from your drive yesterday." I lifted the ball of dough and put it in a greased bowl, then draped a dishtowel over the top and set it aside to rise.

"That was for work. This time I do not drive for work."

A spot low in my stomach flexed like a fist, and my cheek twitched. I busied myself by setting out ingredients for strawberry shortcake. Mattie had told me of Stanley's recent outing to a church ice cream social with a waitress from the café. I had seen the woman's green Pinto drive down the lane to Stanley's house and bring him home five hours later. "Depends on when you need it," I said. "I have to give it an oil change one night this week."

He told me that while I was planting a late row of cabbage, he had changed the oil. I had no other reason to say no. "We can't make this a permanent arrangement. I can't have my truck gone in the evenings."

"I ask only for tonight." He walked to the foyer, making no effort to appear that he had come to visit. He laced up his boots. With one foot on the porch, he turned and said, "You did not ask why I needed the truck."

I shook my head.

"May I pick you up at six?"

I nodded, and he put on his ball cap and smiled as he left.

Rather than wait for Stanley, I drove the truck to his place at six o'clock. He stepped onto his porch shaking his head and chuckling as he crossed his arms. We could have been driving to the John Deere dealer in Wooster, had it not been for his clean pair of jeans and my pale blue blouse. My blouse folded in pleats across the front and dipped low enough that I put on a simple pearl necklace. The necklace had looked misplaced without the matching earrings, so I clipped on the tiny iridescent pearls, which made my face look pale and plain. I quietly opened Mattie's bathroom drawer and touched her palest lipstick to my lips and brushed a bit of powder on my cheeks. I stopped there because I did not know why Stanley was picking me up at six.

Stanley stood by the driver's side looking at me. He tapped on the window, so I rolled it down. The scent of aftershave confirmed that he had shaved for the second time that day.

"I thought I'd save you the walk," I said, casually crossing my hands over the steering wheel. He nodded but did not move toward the other side of the truck, so I asked if I arrived too early.

"Do you know where we go?" he asked. I looked beyond him to the soybean fields. White butterflies fluttered like scraps of paper over the field. I shook my head. "It will be hard for you to drive us then," Stanley said. I slid to the passenger side.

We rode in silence, which felt different from working in silence. He commented on it being the first day of summer. I replied we ought to work on the longest day of the year. He said nothing and turned onto a side road that led to farms and more side roads. I did not tell him that I never worked on the evening of this day, if it could be helped. He had serendipitously chosen this strange outing on my birthday.

Twice, I caught his glance. I tucked my hair behind my ear and asked, "How do I look?"

"Different." He ran his finger along his lips and nodded toward me.

I laughed and teased him about his hair. The comb tracks in his wet, hair-sprayed hair told of the considerable effort he'd taken to keep it off his forehead. On hot summer days, I had seen him pour water over his head and run his hands through his frayed sweep of bangs. They either stuck up straight or spread flat across his forehead. He had a broad strong forehead. I reached over and tugged on a gray hair. He too had moonlit streaks that I noticed for the first time. I almost let my hand rest in the warmth of the back of his neck. He smiled at my teasing.

I drew back my hand. "We need to dig a deeper trench for the weigh scales," I said. I had never, purposefully, touched him.

We discussed the points of digging the old trench deeper or digging a new trench, and I rolled down the window for air. In that moment, I remembered all of the ways I could touch a man.

"Do you plan on taking us anywhere?" I asked. He smiled but would not answer, so I guessed. "You're craving a waffle cone from Becky's." He turned right at the four-way stop. "No? Good. Her tables are always sticky." I tapped my foot. "Charlie's Family Restaurant?" He made a left turn onto Route 17. "Good. Why does he advertise home cooking? Why pay for something you always eat?" He could take us to Mansfield by this route, though he had wasted time and gasoline if that was his plan. "I can't think of a place in Mansfield that isn't overpriced," I said. He smiled.

"You are finished guessing?" When I nodded, he said, "Good." His quick succession of turns confused me. We weren't driving toward Carson or Mansfield. He drove directly to the farm. When we pulled up to the house, he said, "You do not like restaurants or ice cream parlors, no? Mansfield is expensive and so is Carson. So I bring you home."

I jerked the door handle and hopped out quickly. Feeling silly with coated lips, I pressed them to the back of my hand. I unclipped the pearl earrings that pinched my ears and slipped them into my pocket. "Thanks for the drive," I said over my shoulder, so he would not see my disappointment that it wasn't otherwise. He followed me to the house. Before I opened the door, I smelled meat loaf. Mattie ran to the table with two steaming baked potatoes. She turned from the table set for three and smiled. "Happy Birthday."

I disliked Mattie's pictures of that evening. My scrunched up face as she put a hat on me. My balloon face when I blew out the candles. My scowling face when they put a gift in front of me. I tore the pictures in half. I hoped she would remember the evening as I did. I clapped my hands and laughed when they sang "Dottie Connell had a Birthday" to the tune of Old McDonald. "With an uh-ouch here," they sang, as Stanley pretended to walk with an imaginary cane. I smiled when I unwrapped the empty box. My gift, I learned upon walking to the barn, was a purebred Airedale. She jerked from her chain, and I knelt to take the squirming bundle in my lap for a picture. I had unknowingly turned my head when Mattie clicked the shutter.

Chapter Sixteen

By July, all of Mattie's pictures featured the community pool in Mansfield. Half of a rainbow blow-up ball. A snorkel at the bottom of the pool. Fins propped on a lawn chair. A row of mothers' legs on poolside deck chairs. Her friend, Pauline, not only had her driver's license, but she also had a sympathetic older sister home from Ohio University with her used Volkswagen Bug.

Mattie ran through the house each Saturday morning with an energy I never saw in her chores throughout the week. She had a lime green swim bag, the color of weeds and sick plants. The bag smelled exotic from the baby oil to darken her skin and the lemon juice to lighten her hair and from the deeper, musky smells of sweaty, chlorinated skin. Why go to the trouble to pack this bag and waste money on gas, I asked each week, when they could swim in our pond?

"We don't go to swim," Mattie said, as though I should understand this. When I was young, my brother and I ran to the pond as soon as our parents decided it was too hot to give more chores. I could almost smell the coolness of the water as we ran down the hill to the spring-fed pond.

From Mattie's pictures, I learned the city found another use for concrete. I couldn't imagine touching concrete at the bottom of water. It was not natural. Only bits of lawn surrounded the pool. From the pictures it appeared this patch of grass belonged to the teenagers. In the pictures, other lime green bags and other girls, not swimming, scattered the lawn.

I went to the pool one time. I wore a large white cover-up over an old, blue swimsuit that I wore when I swam in my pond on humid afternoons. The cover-up stretched to my knees, and I left it on the entire afternoon. The mothers of the teenage girls also came for reasons other than swimming. Their striped and colorful suits appeared to be designed for the purpose of lying beside the pool. My pilled, faded swimsuit was only appropriate in murky pond water.

Even the lifeguards showed no intention of getting into the water. They wore sunglasses and hats. One even draped a towel over his shoulders. His job was apparently to safeguard the lawn of teenage girls and leave the water-winged youngsters to the other lifeguards. When I arrived, I waved to Mattie and her friends. None of them waved back. I sat in the chair for three hours, an adequate time to justify a thirty-minute drive, and left without telling Mattie good-bye.

Mattie's next roll of film featured a lifeguard, as disembodied as the barn kittens earlier that summer. His whistle dangling from his tanned wrist. His shadow on the sidewalk below his chair. A towel over his shoulders.

The kitchen was hot. Moving only stirred the heat, and sweat dripped from my body even if I stood still. I sliced tomatoes and cheese to eat on buttermilk rolls for supper. I rolled a cloth under cool water and tucked it under my collar as I sliced watermelon. I envied Mattie at the pool; even if she did not swim, a breeze might come off the water.

Pauline beeped the cartoon horn of the VW. Mattie wore a towel around her fuchsia suit, though I had spent grocery money to buy her a cover-up. The pup barked and Mattie cooed and asked her who had tied her to the tree. Named Frisco by Mattie, after San Francisco, the pup jumped in arcs close to back-flips at the attention.

"Don't let her loose," I yelled out the window. The dog lacked good sense. She ran headlong toward sound. I had tied her to the tree until Stanley finished cutting the hay.

A slice of watermelon slipped from my hand. I could not concentrate in the heat. I wiped the floor from the splat of seed and watermelon juice. I did not plan for my conversation with Mattie to be an argument, but it would become one. I worked at cheerfulness that summer. I ignored her new diet of Pepsi and Mallomars and little else. I picked up her clothes from the floor of her bedroom when I did laundry. Our conversations, though strained, were pleasant. But I could not ignore the third roll of film that featured the lifeguard.

Mattie kicked off her sandals in the corner by the door. She munched on blackberries she swiped from the bushes near the house. I told her the pictures were on the table.

I sliced the rolls for the sandwiches and spread mayonnaise on each half of the roll. "Next Saturday we're planting the winter wheat."

"I go to the pool on Saturdays."

"Not in August."

Mattie flipped through the pictures. "You leave smudges."

I lined the tomato slices on a plate. "What?"

"Smudges. Thumbprints. On my pictures."

I placed the cheese slices beside the tomatoes and set the plate on the table in front of Mattie. She looked at her pictures again. "You never ask to see them."

"I pay for them."

"With money that I work for."

"And you will work for the money in August, when there is more work to be done." I brought over the Tupperware bowl full of watermelon slices. Mattie had the pictures of the lifeguard spread in front of her.

"I might see a man at the pool. Is that it?" she asked.

I sat at the table and assembled my sandwich. "We have work to do."

"No school dances, no movies, no swimming pool. If I see them, I might touch them." Her face flushed. She mimicked my voice, "Don't let them touch you, Mattie. Don't let them hold your hand. Even better, stay home and pretend we're best friends, because I can't make any of my own." Mattie watched me. I ate my sandwich and held her gaze. She lowered her voice. "No matter how hard you try, you can't keep me here forever. I will not be a bitter, old virgin like you."

I put down my sandwich and wiped my mouth. Her smug superiority brought a retort to my lips that I would not say. Instead, I told her she knew nothing about my life.

"I know plenty. You're licking twenty-year-old wounds that were your own fault." Mattie leaned her chair against the wall. "Did you kiss him good-bye?"

"Did I? You seem to know the story." I measured the words, so the shaking that ran from my knees to my stomach would not come out in my voice.

"You can't even get angry." She laughed. "Silly me, to think you ever loved anything other than this farm. It's a good thing you didn't kiss him good-bye. He might have thought you loved him. And then what would have happened when he delivered that letter to Charlotte?"

I cut my watermelon into bit-sized pieces, ignoring that Mattie apparently knew more about Morris and Charlotte than I ever had.

"Leave," I said quietly, then louder, "Leave this table."

She did, and I was alone.

By the first week of August, a yellow school bus creaked over the hills and around the turns of the valley. I wondered if Mr. Sheller's replacement practiced the route more for the comfort of the parents than for himself. The prior February, Mr. Sheller had slid on black ice across the road into a snow bank high enough to keep the bus from rolling. Now I waited for the appearance of the bus to spark a new argument that began the day of Mattie's sixteenth birthday. I never loaned her the truck to drive to school, even if I planned to spend the day on my tractor. But she said nothing of the bus or of the new chores that busied her on Saturdays. She washed the dishes without being asked and hung towels and sheets on the line rather than tossing them in the dryer as she often did, acting as if she forgot my preference. Yet she was as smug as if she had won an argument.

Every evening she slung her camera over her shoulder and walked out the door without saying a word. I never saw the pictures. Pauline's sister developed them; "Without looking at them," she said, as if daring me to complain. I tucked the money I budgeted for developing her film into an empty Planter's peanut jar and hid it in my desk drawer. By Christmas I would have almost enough for the tripod she wanted.

Nothing made her smile more than an evening of picture taking. She bristled with an energy I wanted to touch. When I found leaves crushed in her hair, I picked them out before she could brush away my hand. I imagined her on her back snapping a shot of the sky scarred by branches. I missed seeing her pictures.

Buried rubber tires, like secrets, tended to find their way to the surface. It could take twenty or thirty years before a man plowed another man's fallow fields to discover his temporary solution of hiding the tires under earth. Our creations decayed slower than God's. The death of Jim Yates worked like a cultivator across our fields, unearthing a secret Mattie nearly succeeded in keeping from me.

Cancer felled Jim faster than a chainsaw on a sapling. Four and a half months earlier when the doctor gave him five months to live, everyone said he was too sturdy to go down so quickly. Sturdy as an oak, an ox, a bull, I heard them say. But the disease diminished him so quickly he acquired the nickname Slim Jim. He embraced the nickname and even used it when referring to himself. People did not nickname a dying man.

The number of funerals that Evelyn Yates had attended had not prepared her for grief. Over the past twenty years, funerals in the valley had been followed by hearty servings of Evelyn's potato salad heaped alongside Retha's sloppy joes and Alice's sugarless pie. When I called with condolences, Evelyn sounded stunned without piles of potatoes to peel in response to her husband's death, or so I told Retha when she recruited me to make the potato salad in Evelyn's place. When I asked Retha if it might do Evelyn good to chop potatoes, she said, "Really, Dottie. If it's that much trouble, I'll ask someone else."

Retha nearly hung up on me when I asked why any gathering needed ten pounds of potato salad. "Because with their mouths full, they don't have to think of anything to say, so they eat more," she said. So I chopped ten pounds of potatoes, fifteen boiled eggs, nine stalks of celery, and twenty-four dill pickle spears, stirred in two and a quarter cups of mayonnaise, and worried that I had somehow taken something from Evelyn.

Mattie could not have anticipated Jim Yates's death any more than she could have known that Evelyn's cousin was her boyfriend's mother. She could not have known that the funeral's attendees would discuss family trees to identify each person's proximity to Jim's death, nor that when I told a woman I was only a neighbor that she would ask if I knew a delightful young woman, Mattie Morgan.

On the evening Mattie's boyfriend came for supper, she spent the day in the kitchen, shooing me away as soon as

I offered to grill burgers to eat with the leftover potato salad from the funeral. She knew better than to deny his existence. When I told her to bring him home for supper, she only asked who told me. I knew better than to get angry. I understood, as God must have, that forbidding hastened action.

She had borrowed a Betty Crocker cookbook from Pauline's mother and bookmarked the pork crown roast with mushroom stuffing, Roquefort and toasted walnut salad, rosemary roasted potatoes, and Boston crème pie. I handed her the keys to the truck and told her she wouldn't find any ingredients for those recipes in the house. By two o'clock the kitchen reminded me of my mother's herb garden in August, when the sun mingled the scent of sage, thyme, and rosemary. By four o'clock nearly every spatula and pan that I owned filled the sink. I set to washing them, and Mattie said nothing as she tried to fill the nearly cooked roast with stuffing.

"Is he always this hard to please?" I asked, as I rinsed a pot.

"I've never cooked for him before."

"For your sake, I hope you don't plan on cooking for him again. You'll never live up to this."

"Do you have to hang the pot over the stove?" she asked as I dried it. "It's not a tool shed."

When I finished drying, I stacked the pans and carried them into the basement. Mattie had caused, with the same swiftness, other changes in the house. A new floral couch, lavender carpet in her bedroom, goldenrod countertops in the kitchen. She rarely demanded improvements, yet she shocked me each time with a disdain that neared hate.

I set the pans in the basement on shelves above my mother's cedar chest filled with her linens. As my mother's health declined, she had wrapped her crocheted tablecloths and linen napkins in layers of tissue paper as if swathing them for burial. She knew I would never use them. This rare acceptance of our differences pained me. I opened the chest and unwrapped three napkins and a tablecloth and then took them outside to air them.

It was a still afternoon with an almost imperceptible breeze that kept the heat of August from settling on the skin. August brides prayed for this weather. I spread the tablecloth across the picnic table in the backyard and checked it for spots. A fist-sized blotch of yellow stained its center where my mother's vases once sat. I found a pot in the garage and with my knife cut clumps of lavender from my mother's perennial garden that had grown wild. I took the pot to the pond and scooped muck and water to hold the lanky flowers in place and then set the pot filled with flowers in the center of the table. I would take it inside to see if Mattie wanted me to set the dining room table.

"I like it," Mattie yelled from the window.

"Inside or outside?"

"Outside. He likes the pond," she yelled.

I waved and folded three napkins. On my way to the house, I circled the pond. Sure enough. Two sets of footprints marked their walk around the edge and then into the pond. What had she told him about me that he came so close to my house without meeting me?

By the time Travis's car kicked up dirt on the lane, Mattie hid the evidence of her efforts. Two dishtowels covered the roast pan soaking in the sink. She let down her ponytail and combed her fingers through her hair. I glimpsed the nervousness that must have preceded their first conversation, first date, first kiss.

Travis knocked even though he could have called to us through the screen door. He had a polite stance. He held his hands loosely in front of him. When I opened the door, he extended his hand, and we exchanged a firm shake. He was the type of boy fathers liked.

He was more tan than handsome. His skin had the warmth of a perfectly ripened peach. His smile distracted one from studying his protruding ears or his mat of tight blond curls. Yet I found myself watching Mattie more than Travis as we carried the meal outside. They walked in step, familiar with the other's stride. Mattie appeared more womanly in the slight sway of her hips, in the easy way she touched his arm as she walked into a slight dip in the yard. She smiled slower with a wiser expression than when she giggled with Trudy and Pauline. She smiled like Zela.

I prayed for blessing over the food. Outdoors in the palm of the valley, my faith that God may listen surged for a moment until I looked on my fields, my source of faith and doubt. They prospered with or without prayers and failed with or without them as well. Even if God heard my prayers, I saw no point in praying for what I could do myself. But I prayed for His blessing on every meal, because Mattie once asked me to.

"Did you finish your chores?" Travis laughed as he asked Mattie. She playfully cuffed his arm and passed him the Roquefort and walnut salad.

"I didn't get a minute from her," I said. "She seemed to think this meal was the most important thing today." I smiled and handed him the rolls.

"I want to hear about farmer Mattie," he said, as he rubbed his hand on her knee. Mattie's leg did not twitch at his caress. His hand rested as easy as a saddle on a horse that had been broken. Her body knew his hands. How had I not seen this in her eyes?

"Did she really milk cows?" he asked.

"Hardly," I said.

Mattie gasped, "I hadn't been here three days before she had me milking cows."

"I wouldn't call what she did in those days milking."

"Then I wouldn't call what you did mothering," Mattie said. Her grin was more playful than her words.

"That's fair," I said to Travis. "I didn't know what else to do with an eight-year-old than to teach her how to milk."

"So she did milk."

"Eventually. For all of her complaining, I believe she was sad the day we sold the last cow."

"Now that shows how bad her memory is," Mattie said to Travis. "Stanley and I went on a milk strike and told her pouring milk on her cereal and a splash in her coffee wasn't worth getting up at six in the morning."

Travis laughed as if he had not heard of our quarrels. Mattie's laughter, for a moment, made our tension something of the past. I laughed with them.

"Do you have an interest in farming?" I asked and then regretted it. They both stopped laughing. I had blurted my greatest hope aloud before Mattie had passed the roast. From Travis's expression, I saw he would not be my ally in convincing Mattie to stay.

"Or maybe working at the steel mill with your father?" I asked, hoping to salvage the moment with the only bit of information I learned from his mother at the funeral. Mattie's frown revealed I had misspoken. "Your father does work at the steel mill?" I asked.

"Third shift. He says he likes sleeping in the daytime because he feels like he's getting away with something. Neither would suit me," he said. "They're both here, which is only the first thing wrong with them."

We passed the roast and then the potatoes. He complimented them both before tasting them. Mattie lied and said it was nothing. I felt too old to chew. I had watched this couple thirty years earlier in the Brubakers' dining room. I had failed Mattie. How could she show so little imagination? She could have found more original ways to leave this valley.

"So when you graduate, where do you plan to go?"

He glanced at Mattie as if his answer could betray her. "I'm going to the University of Southern California this fall."

I nearly grinned at this answer. "So you're leaving in a couple of weeks."

He told me he chose USC for its theater department. I hardly listened to him but asked as many questions as I could so that the reality of his departure would be obvious to Mattie. He would break her heart, and I would comfort her.

"It all started when I acted in the school musicals. For a few hours every day, I could live in River City, Iowa or Oklahoma. I plan to end up in Hollywood."

When I asked him if he really believed he could act in movies, he heard the real question in my voice.

"I'm not good-looking enough to be a leading man, but they need sidekicks to make them look handsome."

Mattie laughed. "I don't think she's ever been to the movies."

I could laugh again, and for the next half hour Travis told me about *Cabaret* and *The Godfather*. He knew directors' middle names and how Bob Rafelson and Albert S. Ruddy got their first breaks. He knew actors' names like I knew trees. He told stories about Paul Winfield, Peter O'Toole, and James Caan.

He would forget Mattie as soon as classes began. Only when I sliced the pie did he pause and ask, "Wasn't Stanley going to join us?"

Mattie nodded and then said to me, "I told him he should join us for dessert. He wants to meet Travis." I nodded as if I knew of this plan and slid my unused spoon across the table so he would have silverware for dessert. Mattie took her time walking toward Stanley's, causing me to hesitate with what I planned to say to Travis. She trusted me with him. She trusted him that their relationship would not end. Once she was out of sight, I told him what I believed he should know. I explained why Mattie was not to be trusted.

Chapter Seventeen

Flecks of grass freckled my body. They tickled the inside of my ear and crawled down my collar. My arms shook as if I still held the wheel of the mower. I had mowed five acres of lawn, a task I wished I could avoid by planting soybeans around my house and barn. A shower, a meal, and a crossword puzzle were my plans for the evening. My new routine over the past week had left me vaguely dissatisfied that Mattie no longer hid her evenings with Travis. He came for her earlier and returned her later.

She neglected her chores now that she did not need the diversion. I glanced out the window. No towels hung on the line. Towels with the electric smell from the dryer would be more tolerable than finding them still in the washing machine.

Focused on finding water-heavy towels, I hardly noticed when I stepped into a puddle at the bottom of the stairs. The suction of my shoes in shallow water seemed a vague premonition of what I would find in the washing machine, not what I expected walking across my basement. The empty washer provided a false hope, but the dryer was empty as well. Mattie had not even brought down the armload of dirty towels.

Only then did I realize I stood in a half-inch of water. "For Pete's sake," I said, as I splashed through the room, tugging the cotton strings dangling from the four bulb lights. My voice echoed loud and lonely off the painted cinderblock walls of the basement. I kicked the indoor-outdoor carpet, sending a light spray of water from the toe of my boot.

Water stained a wide river across the brown carpet. Its broad tributaries stretched to the corners of the basement. The water was frantic in its efforts to return to the soil. After last night's storm had passed, a heavy smell of life had lingered in the air, but that same rain smelled stagnant in the dank basement, overlaid by the smell of mold already taking root.

This was the second time this summer the drain clogged. After trying to flush it out with the hose, I decided not to bother with the snake, which before had only partially loosened the heavy mat of roots that had broken through the pipe. Back in July I knew I should replace this portion of the pipeline.

Still wearing my mowing clothes, I fired up the backhoe and drove it six feet from the back of the house where I first laid the pipe and scratched a four-foot trench above it. Wiry roots jutted into the hole from a spruce eight feet west of the trench—the roots defiant in their attempt to hold the tree firm without dirt. With a pickaxe I set to uncovering whatever jolted the backhoe before it hit the pipe. By the time I reached a layer of rocks wedged around the pipe, dusk cast its yellow shadows through my trees, their trunks already black as night.

Frisco looked into the dark as if someone approached us. When she did not bother to bark or scramble toward the shadows, I knew Stanley was near. I stood in the hole working out rocks that nearly twenty years earlier I dropped easily into the trench as fill. Stanley knelt near me and surveyed the pipe, now exposed like a fractured bone. I tossed another rock onto the pile.

"Seemed like a good spot for the rocks at the time," I said.

"Of course, you do not ask for help," Stanley said, as he rose to his feet and circled the trench. "You are something." His voice did not reveal if he spoke with irritation or admiration.

My arms ached and shook as I lifted the rocks. The jagged edges cut into my fingers as I hoisted them. The muscles in my back tightened in pain. This was a job I should give to Stanley, but I dropped these rocks in, and I would dig them out. He climbed into the trench even though I did not ask him to help me.

The shadows slid into the pockets of light until we worked in darkness. We continued shoveling, tapping the ground, like unfamiliar lovers, for the sound of the pipe before we thrust the shovel into the surrounding earth and lifted it overhead to the ground, now at shoulder level. We stood at opposite ends of the ditch and said nothing as we worked. The thrum and trill of the frogs at the edge of the pond did not hide the silence between us. I sensed Stanley's disapproval from the speed of his work. He worked faster when he disagreed with me, as if finishing the job was the only way to escape me. Twice I hit the pipe with my shovel, the shock reverberating in my back molars.

"We can't replace a pipe we can't see," Stanley finally said.

"The floodlight should help." I balanced myself on the pipe to crawl out of the trench. I felt Stanley's hand on my back steadying me. The pressure, too light to push me from the trench, was not the firm grip of one of us offering the other a hand. It was so slight it felt like care.

My arms shook from exhaustion as I flipped on the kitchen light and the floodlight behind the house. The screen door banged shut behind Stanley as he entered the kitchen.

"Thirsty?" I asked.

He motioned toward the chair. "Sit down."

"I'll put on some coffee for us."

"You walked up the hill like this." He swayed and then took an unsteady step forward.

"Staggered," I said, so accustomed to our language charades, I thought more about the word than what he had said.

"Yes, you staggered." He pulled back a chair from the kitchen table. "You have not had supper?"

I looked at the clock. At half past nine, I should have eaten supper, but only a dull hunger reminded me of my evening that started with wanting a clean towel for my shower. I shook my head.

"I did not think so."

Opening the refrigerator, he found a package of bologna and a chunk of cheese behind the milk jug. He lifted tinfoil off a Cool Whip container. "Macaroni salad," I said. He ran his hand over the bottles in the side of the refrigerator until he found a jelly jar of dill pickles and bottles of ketchup and mustard. I felt too tired to object.

Rolling his shirt-sleeves past his elbows, he wiped his muddy hands on a towel without running them under water. Half of the package of bologna created the base of the sandwich. He chunked half-inch slices of cheese, lathered the ketchup and mustard liberally over a small heap of pickles, and then added a quartered tomato and a thin layer of sliced cucumber on top.

"And you complained about my eggs," I finally said with a grin.

"I work with what I have here." He smiled and set the sandwich and the macaroni salad in front of me.

"That doesn't mean every ingredient in my refrigerator should be on one sandwich." I laughed.

We never shared meals alone inside my house. Culling the woods, we had gulped water from a shared jug or sat on a fallen log to eat our sandwiches, but Mattie's vacant chair made me aware of the emptiness of the house. I had never felt so alone with Stanley.

"Mattie should be home by now," I said, as if her name would fill the house with her. Instead, I felt our aloneness more. We rarely sat this close without a task, and I felt every inch of the kitchen table that separated us. I relaxed my fingers and spread them as if I could touch the warmth between us.

Stanley stared at me. How did we manage to work side by side without seeing each other's eyes? His eyes always reminded me of a murky stream, and now I saw why.

Flecks of brown and green muddied his blue eyes. The skin at the corner of his eyes puckered with wrinkles like a stitch tugged too tightly. A fine crease ran along his left cheek, but not his right, from his habit of a lopsided grin. As he studied my face, I wondered which wrinkles he noticed first. His expression spoke more fluently than he ever could. Only Morris had ever looked at me with eyes as sleepy with desire. My cheeks flushed, and my face felt softer, prettier, than it was.

"I've seen that waitress at your place," I said, though I had intended never to raise the subject. I needed to splash cold water between us.

"Not often," he said. "We're good for each other's loneliness. Nothing more."

"I doubt she sees it that way," I said. "Women rarely do."

Chewing the first bite of his sandwich, he studied me. I looked down at my plate, not wanting to fall back into the rushing water of his eyes.

"It is not that way," he said. "She is loyal to another man. She tells me about this man, who is married. He breaks her heart, but she cannot break his heart."

"Her skirts are short enough to break any man's heart."

He laughed and swiped his mouth with a napkin. "Men can always find women who wear short skirts. These women cannot break a man's heart."

"I never knew you to be so experienced in these matters," I said. This talk was drawing us to a place that could ruin every silence we ever shared, so before he could reply I said, "I didn't know I was so hungry. I forget I need to eat."

"I think you forget many things."

I took another bite of my sandwich and refused to look at him. "You should have left this farm years ago."

Sitting back in his chair, he snapped a cord between us. He bit into his sandwich and chewed vigorously. I eased back in my chair and ate a few mouthfuls of salad. "I'm not saying you haven't helped this farm. I'm saying this farm hasn't helped you."

"I have a place to sleep and outdoor work. This is what I asked for."

"You don't have anything to call your own. You're not a young man. Don't you want land and a family?"

"I had a farm with my brother. We could have shared it if I made different choices."

"You left your land?"

"My brother asked me to."

"You left without a fight?"

He rubbed the back of his neck and tilted back in his chair. The legs of the chair thumped on the linoleum as he stood and poured himself a glass of milk.

"So you did," I said.

"I do not want to talk about this. It ended badly."

I could feel us sliding back toward the silence that filled our work. Tomorrow we could blame our words on our tiredness or Mattie's absence, but we would not speak of this again. When he first arrived and proved himself reliable, I had not needed to know. Now I could not fully understand why I wanted to know. "Why did you leave your country?" I asked.

"Why have you never married?"

I laughed at the swiftness of his response as if these two questions always existed between us, one ready to counter whoever asked first. He came back to the table and swiveled the chair on one leg.

"The decision isn't entirely up to me."

"And when has this ever stopped you?"

"I don't follow you."

He shrugged as if he could not explain himself any better than he had.

"You think I would be married if I wanted to."

"You take a shovel to rock in the dark. Nothing stops you."

"And you leave land simply because someone asks you to, so what should I assume about you?"

Stanley leaned into the back of the chair and rested his chin on his crossed arms. Finally he said, "My brother and I loved the same woman. He asked me to leave."

"So you abandoned your land and your woman, because he asked you to."

"That is right."

"I suppose she married the man willing to fight for her."

"She was already his wife," he said.

"You lost your land for a woman?"

"I lost my family for a woman."

"Your brother had every right to his wife, but not to your land."

Stanley shook his head as if I misunderstood him. His eyes had a strange look of pity. "I never wanted the land."

"Ten years ago I wouldn't have believed you."

"And now?"

"I believe you, but I don't understand you," I said. "I can't believe a man would choose to spend ten years without land or a woman."

"I made a mistake with my brother's wife. She accused me of terrible things."

"Were they true?"

"They became true when more people believed her instead of me."

"What did she say?"

Stanley shook his head and stood up. He propped his foot on the chair, tied the laces that he had loosened under the table, and turned the chair back into its place. "What she said when we were alone was different from what she said to my brother. She told me she would do this. If he caught us, she would say she never spoke love to me. But when she told me she loved me, I did not care. But she did worse than deny her love." He paused and shook his head. "I will never take a woman in my arms again unless she asks me to. I will never ask again."

This talk could only lead to conversations I did not want to have with Stanley. I wanted to shake the feeling that I owed him a story of my own now. "I kept us up too late. You should get some rest." I recovered the dried out macaroni salad, crimping the foil around the edge as if I worked a piecrust.

I drizzled a few drops of soap on the plates in the sink and splashed my hand under the water until it felt as warm as his hand on my back. As I filled the sink with hot, soapy water, Stanley walked toward the door. The warmth on my back lingered, like the heat of the truck gusting on my feet, leaving the rest of me aching for warmth. I turned toward the door, and Stanley stopped as if I called his name.

"This is why you did not marry," he said. "A man needs to feel useful. Let me help with the dishes."

"We have plenty of work early tomorrow. After we replace the pipe, one of us will have to mop out the swamp in the basement." I was slipping into the familiar place where I knew how to talk to him. "I'll need your help in the morning."

"Let me help," he said again. I stiffened as he came toward me, remembering how I should feel around a hired man. He stood so close to me I could reach for him or hand him the dishtowel.

Gravel pinged on the belly of Travis's car. I glanced at the clock and realized Mattie was two hours late. Stanley looked at me as he had when we came into the house.

Travis's car creaked to a slow stop. Even though they were late, Mattie would kiss him goodnight. In the time it took her to kiss him, I could lean into Stanley. I could ask him to put his arms around me. He had not stepped toward or away from me. I stepped back, distrusting my desire, and outside Mattie slammed shut the car door.

She did not come through the kitchen, but struggled with the front door until it groaned open and, without saying hello, stumbled up the stairs. Slamming her bedroom door did not hide the sound of her sobbing.

"Go to her," Stanley said, and then he left.

As I hoed her garden, I kept an eye toward Mattie's window. When I reached the rows of peas, I snapped open a grocery bag. I broke pea pods from the vines with two hands and tossed the fistfuls into the bag beside me. The crisp juice of broken pods stained my fingers with its smell. Stanley chopped trees for new fence posts. The echo had the sound of a dog's bark on distant farms.

When Mattie woke, I would tell her that she was grounded. I picked the peas as an attempt at a truce before her punishment. I did not want her to resent the farm as a place of confinement.

After hoeing the garden and lining the picnic bench by the door with tomatoes, squash, and peppers, I shelled the peas. I had risen at five in the morning to lay the pipe alone and planned to join Stanley in fashioning the fence posts, but it felt awkward to see him. Daylight would cast an embarrassing shadow on how I felt the night before. At three in the afternoon, Mattie was still sleeping. I went inside to cook the peas for supper and was glad that afternoon afforded a reason to work apart from Stanley.

The kitchen was dark. I saw the glow of the gas burner on the stove, and then I saw Mattie sitting at the kitchen table drinking coffee. I flicked on the lights, though I often cooked without them to keep the kitchen cool. Mattie blinked but did not shade her eyes. She wore her flannel winter pajamas, though it was ninety degrees in the shade. Nothing sat on the red-hot stove burner.

"Trying to burn down the house?" I snapped off the burner. The kitchen was stifling. Mattie had closed the windows. I fanned myself. Heat crept up my back and my neck. I shoved open the windows.

Mattie stared at the tree outside the window. Corncobs jutted from nails like ladder rungs up the trunk. A squirrel nibbled nervously. A bird flew against the windowpane. "That crazy bird," I said, rubbing a napkin over my neck. Mattie did not laugh as we often did when a bird crashed into its reflection.

"Got no more sense than that dog," I said. "Stanley nearly ran over Frisco this morning. She doesn't learn."

I took the orange juice from the refrigerator. "Which hurts worse, your head or your pride?" When I knocked the night before, she had not opened her door, so I didn't doubt she wanted to hide the result of a few too many beers. I stirred a teaspoon of lime juice and a pinch of cumin in the orange juice and told her to drink it. "Coffee won't help."

I pulled a chair close to hers. She did not wince when I gave her the orange juice, so I asked her if her stomach could handle eggs. She shook her head.

"What charade were you pulling last night?" She had her mother's eyes. I had seen this sorrow in Zela's eyes, sorrow for what would come rather than what had been. But I had confused the two.

"You can quit worrying about your punishment," I said. "You're grounded. But there's no reason to mope about it. You're not the first person to stumble home to this house."

When she did not argue with me, I said, "You might as well tell Travis that he can't bring you home that late and expect to see you."

"He isn't planning on seeing me again."

That afternoon I cooked her a breakfast that had once been her favorite. I grated cheese and thawed bacon. I whisked eggs and sliced shortening into flour. Nearly humming, I sprinkled flour on the counter and flopped the biscuit dough on its grainy surface. I poured a liberal amount of bacon gravy over the biscuits and scooped a heap of cheese-covered eggs next to it. Mattie had not moved as I worked. This was a time to care for her. This was my chance to get it right. When she asked for another round of biscuits and gravy, I no longer regretted what I had said to Travis.

Chapter Eighteen

September was a time of gathering up, bringing things indoors. The garden now sat in jars in neat rows on shelves in the basement. Mattie and I spent every evening boiling Mason jars and filling them with anything we had not already canned in August. We sliced apples and dropped them slippery as minnows into the jars. Cucumbers soaked in vinegar. Tomatoes stewed. The house smelled of Sunday dinners every evening, and the farm smelled of harvest. Stanley and I checked and rechecked engines and belts. We prepared the grain bins. We bided our time until the corn harvest.

This season tempted me to pray. Other farmers prayed in the spring when the rain continued too long or in the summer when the rain stopped. I nearly avoided the thought of God in those seasons. But harvest terrified me. I knew by September what my crops could yield, and only then did my fears surface. I never prayed for God's help in what I could do myself, but occasionally my prayers joined with others in the valley for the weather. For a moment, these prayers drifted no farther than the puff of cold air that trailed from my mouth as I prayed, "Don't let it snow." The heaviness of the silence that followed the prayers felt as immense as God. I couldn't say what I expected to hear. But the silence settled on me like an accusation, and in those moments I believed there was a God.

The Mansfielders who came for berries in the summer bought our firewood in the fall. Stanley and I culled the woods for ash, wild cherry, and red elm. This dry wood did not have to sit as long in their garages. I had given up explaining green wood that was not green. Stanley took armloads of wood and stacked them in cords under the shelter near the road. People could drive up in their borrowed trucks and pick up the wood without interrupting our work.

The chain saw puttered as I lifted my goggles and wiped the sweat from my eyes. Stanley leaned over the pile and tossed the logs into the wheelbarrow.

"I worry for Mattie," he said without stopping his work.

"Worried that she finally took to farm work?" I asked.

"In part. She has lost her smile."

I pulled the string of the chain saw and popped my goggles back in place. We had work to finish. "She's fine," I yelled over the roar and severed another log in two. I did not have time for false worries. Mattie had never taken to farm work as she had since she stopped seeing Travis. She crawled her way through the green bean rows, plucking the last beans of the season. She shucked corn standing and leveraged her whole weight into ripping husks from the cobs. In the evenings, she ran the path of my winter walks up the hill to the back forty. She worked until her face turned pale, and she nearly heaved from the exertion. I recognized it all. It was the only way for a woman to forget a man, to work the feel of him out of her skin.

"Can you hear me?" Stanley cupped his hand to his mouth. I placed my hand to my ear and shook my head. I put another log on the block.

"Mattie misses school in the morning, and I take her. She is unhappy," he yelled. I shrugged my shoulders as if his words flew past me like the dust from the cut logs.

"You are not an easy woman to love, Dottie Connell, but I do."

I kept my head down and tossed the logs onto the pile beside me. I cut the wood faster, angered that he could say the words so easily. He could not mean words that he tossed out with the ease that he loaded logs into the truck. I refused to look at him. He piled the truck bed high with logs. As he shut the door, he yelled from the open window, "I know you hear me."

The corn rained from the combine into the hopper. A few stray kernels pinged like hail against the window of the cab. I wiped my forehead with my handkerchief, though it was November, and it was night. My father had plowed and harvested this soil by daylight. He walked behind his horse and plow and stopped to pick up arrowheads or notice a bird's nest. The lights of the combine set my way by two beams. I could pick up to a hundred and eighty bushels an acre on a good year, and this was a good year. Stanley waited in the tractor to drive the hopper to the drier. He waved for me to finish for the night.

"We've almost finished the field," I yelled. He nodded before I gave the answer he expected. If other valley farmers worked until dusk, I worked until the moon was suspended as high as the noon sun and dew dampened the crops. Stanley drove the hopper to the drier, and I finished the bottom field.

My hips cracked as I walked back to the house. I had sat for fourteen hours, stopping only when Mattie drove sandwiches and a thermos of tomato soup to the field and when I walked stiff-legged to the maple sugar shack's bathroom. I was happy with the ache that came from working past tiredness. The great fans of the drier whirred. I smiled at the sound. We would finish the fields by the following night. Even Mattie's quietness did not bother me. She slept the sleep of hard work. I was proud of her.

She waited for me in the kitchen. Her eyelids puffed with the need for sleep. Pie, corn muffins, and olives were spread on the table. Work had given her an appetite she'd never had in her idleness. She looked heftier yet healthier.

"Save any for me?" I asked. I hung my hat on the peg by the door and unlaced my boots. Gravy-covered dishes in the sink explained the smell of sautéed onions. "Did you make the pork roast?"

She nodded and asked about the harvest. I still answered her questions waiting for her to tell me the real reason she took sudden interest in the farm. I cut slices of cold pork roast and fixed it on three buttermilk rolls with mayonnaise.

"I'll take you to school later in the day tomorrow if you're tired."

Mattie shrugged. "It doesn't make any difference."

"There's no need for you to hide skipping classes. You've worked hard, and that matters more than getting to school on time," I said and, feeling generous, added, "You can skip the whole day if you feel like it. We've done good work."

"I turn eighteen soon," she said, as I took the first bite of my sandwich. She wrapped both hands around her full glass of milk and held on tightly.

I smiled at my plan to throw her a birthday party. I would order the cake with lavender flowers from the Supervalu. The flowers would match the invitations with the scalloped edges that reminded me of lace on a dress Mattie loved as a girl. I started the guest list on the first day of school by asking Mattie whom she had been happy to see.

"Yes, you do," I said.

"Uncle Morris told me I get an inheritance when I turn eighteen."

"And you're not eighteen yet." My words fluttered out with no time to consider them. I cocked my head as though I had uttered wisdom. I couldn't swallow my next bite.

"Why didn't you tell me about it?"

"There's nothing to tell. Your mother gave me money to raise you, and I raised you."

"Uncle Morris said the money was mine."

"Isn't he always meddling." I folded the napkin on my lap into a square. "Your mother left it in my name."

The clock ticked in our silence. I had planned words for this conversation but not for this moment. "I have an inheritance for you, but we'll discuss it when you're old enough for it to be yours," I said.

"I'm old enough to need the money."

"You've never been in want here," I said, as a warmth gathered below my breasts, spreading at first like anger but settling in my stomach like fear. Afraid of her reply, I asked, "Do you want to go shopping this weekend? We could drive to that mall in Columbus that you and Pauline were gabbing about."

"It moved today," Mattie said quietly.

"What did?"

"I didn't think it could take if you overexerted yourself."

Realizing something would change forever as soon as she explained herself, I settled into her pause.

"The book said not to overexert yourself, so I did, but it didn't work," she said. "The baby moved today."

My insides jerked like when my tractor stalled. A baby. Inside her seventeen-year-old body. After only six months of knowing him.

"I'm four months pregnant," she said, as if I had not understood her.

I slapped her. My hand caught her jaw instead of her cheek. She turned her face from me, her dark hair shielding her. I held my stinging hand tightly to my chest, feeling my heart beat through my turtleneck and flannel shirt. The room snapped into focus as if I had drowsily walked through it since childhood. The harsh light above the kitchen table cast yellow shadows on the lazy Susan in the middle of the table, which was cluttered with vitamin bottles, a plastic bread loaf stuffed with cardboard verses that Mattie once brought home from Sunday school, and a pile of napkins. The place mats curled from their backing. Mattie, round and feminine, her cheeks red with fury, was a stranger to me.

"After all I told you." I sighed as if I had held my breath from the moment Zela brought her to me.

"What did you tell me?"

"I told you everything my mother never dreamed to tell me. But you spread your legs for the first boy who asked you to."

Mattie stiffened, her eyes alert for more. She was poised to argue. "I wanted to know why it scared you. Something made you too scared to love anybody, and I won't live like that."

Mattie never seemed as womanly as she did now. She cradled her belly in her arms, pulling her T-shirt against her. Though a mere bump, it suggested fervent whispers, lips on flesh, willingness. My own skin felt crumpled and barren of any touch that ever brought me to life. This was how she saw me.

"I should have run him off before he ruined you."

"You tried that."

I hesitated. "What did he tell you?"

"That you didn't want us together."

"I told him what his good sense should have. You're looking for a cheap ride out of town. Who gives it makes little difference."

Mattie looked out the window, which merely mirrored our reflection against the darkness of midnight.

"So this is why you came home crying?" I asked. "He won't have anything to do with you now?"

"I left him. He doesn't know about the baby. He said he would marry me after graduation, but I told him he couldn't really love me and leave me here another year. I won't tell him about the baby. Not if you give me my inheritance. You couldn't have spent everything my mother left me."

"What foolishness do you have planned?"

"Pauline's sister went to a home in Akron. I can finish high school there." Her lips flattened into a frown that she inherited from Zela. Ten years of raising Mattie had not made her mine. She could turn from me and from this valley as easily as her mother had.

"I spent your inheritance on this farm. It's our farm. There's no need for you to go off to Akron. You can have the baby here. Between the two of us we can run this farm and raise the baby." As I said this, I knew how badly I wanted it. I wanted the baby to be a boy, so I could carry him on my shoulders into the fields and let him taste dirt before he could crawl. I wanted him to run the trails in the woods as my brother had. I wanted to try again.

Mattie jerked back from me and sucked in a short breath as if I had slapped her again. Shaking her head, she gripped her milk glass with both hands as if holding herself up. Then before I could dodge the throw, she flung her milk glass to the right of me. The full glass of milk splattered down the front of my shirt, soaking through the flannel. The glass hit the wall with a denting thud and fell in large chunks. The cool liquid ran in small streams over my skin and between my breasts. Rather than dabbing up the milk, I held Mattie's gaze as it shifted from confusion to contempt. I would remain calm. I must remain calm. I had imagined this moment for too many years for it not to end as I had planned.

"You spent everything my mother left me? On your farm?" Mattie stood and gripped the top rung of the ladder-back chair.

"You're looking at it wrong. It's ours. It's yours," I said. "I hardly wanted to tell you this way, but this land, all three hundred acres of it, is all yours. You never have to worry that anyone will take it from you."

"It's your farm. I never wanted to live here," she said slowly. She smoothed her shirt over her stomach, resting her hand on the baby. "And I would never let you raise my child. When I look back on this, I'll know this happened to me because I wanted more than anything not to be you."

I could not catch my breath. Only hours before, Mattie had brought me sandwiches in the field. I watched her face for a slight softening of her expression, something to reassure me that I misunderstood the quiet hatred in her words. But she stared, without flinching, with an expression I did not recognize as hers or her mother's. I saw myself.

By the time Stanley came to the house the next morning, I had stopped yelling from the front porch for Mattie. I sat at the kitchen table holding a coffee cup full of coffee gone cold. I already jimmied the lock of Mattie's door, not sure what I would find. Her dresser drawers and closet were empty. The flowered suitcases from Morris and Charlotte at Christmas were gone. I could not think of Mattie dragging her suitcases down the lane to meet the taxi by the mailbox, but I knew she had. The headlights of a taxi on the lane would have reflected off of my bureau mirror. Mattie had also emptied my purse of all its cash and jimmied the lock of the desk drawer and taken the money from the blueberry and firewood sales that I meant to deposit as soon as we finished the harvest.

Well into the night, I had listened to the floorboards creak as Mattie paced the length of her room. I lay in bed, my limbs heavy with her words. But I had not gone to Mattie. She would not hear my words. But I listened for her steps and hoped that she would come to my door.

The next morning Stanley knocked on the side door and came in when I did not answer. "I decided my friend died in her sleep. She works the farm if she is sick. She works the farm if it is cold, if it is dark. Nothing but death would keep her from finishing the harvest. But here she sits, drinking coffee."

"Mattie's gone," I said. I tried to ignore the familiarity of this absence, this betrayal. Something in my chest gaped like soil that holds the shape of a removed stone. I knew how to fill this hole. I would finish the harvest.

Stanley stood and took my hand. He tried to help me to my feet, but I would not move. "We will find her," he said.

"She left on her own will, and she knows her way home if she changes her mind."

"She left?" He sank into the chair and, for a moment, sorrow twisted through me. And then, as if by will, it stopped, and I was barren of feeling. I cleared my throat and swept crumbs from our late-night supper from the place mats.

"So we find her and ask why," he said.

I stared out the window, noting the temperature, watching the squirrels sitting on the cobs of corn stuck in the tree. The squirrel nibbled a kernel and glanced about with the quickness of each bite. The soft sun of coming winter would give the perfect day for harvest.

"She doesn't want to live here. I'm giving her what she wants." Then I put words to the unspoken current that had passed between Mattie and me the night before. I tested the idea by saying it to see if it was true. "I never cared for her," I said.

Chapter Nineteen

By February, the ringing of the telephone still startled me, and it was unsettling to realize that even now I hoped to hear Mattie's voice. I hesitated when the phone rang because twice I had answered it only to realize that I had imagined the ringing.

No one called for Mattie in the days after she left. Not Pauline nor Trudy, not Morris nor Travis. I realized that everyone else knew where she was. When my neighbors did not ask where Mattie had gone, it was clear they assumed I did not know. After a week even Stanley stopped asking if Mattie had called, but I couldn't bring myself to ask him what he knew. It would require an admission to him I could not yet make.

One Saturday, in Mattie's seventh month, I slipped into the library without waving hello to the librarians. Looking in the card catalogue for a book on pregnancy, I flipped nervously through the *p* cards, saying too loudly to a woman next to me that my peas had not fared well this past summer. When I asked her if she gardened, she didn't look up from her card, and I felt more awkward for lying to a stranger about the state of my peas. I retreated to a back corner with the book on pregnancy, embarrassed that someone might recognize a hope that I hardly confessed to myself, a hope that Mattie would return before she birthed this baby.

According to the book, Mattie's baby was already accustomed to where he lived. A dull glow was his dawn. The amniotic fluid subtly changed taste with Mattie's food. He could listen for familiar sounds. He was already learning a life away from the farm.

A sentimental urge to pray came, not in the evenings when silence and shadows filled the kitchen, but in the mornings when I walked through the woods. I nearly prayed for Mattie's return on those morning walks, though she had never risen at six in the morning to hike with me on the ATV trails cut and packed down by the Hilliard boys between our properties. In the mornings, I walked the land that wouldn't need clearing unless Mattie returned. By her graduation I had planned to clear another thirty acres near the back forty. Eventually, I told myself, Mattie would meet a boy grateful to inherit three hundred acres, and I would clear the bottom forty acres before their wedding. And maybe one of their children would follow me, as I tried to follow my father, on the paths between the fields. This child would love the land in a way his mother never could. For this I almost prayed.

By Mattie's eighth month, I could not shake the feeling that she was in Akron with money from Morris. In two months Zela's grandchild could be adopted and live too far from this valley to ever know that he was once a Brubaker. He would never understand why he planted gardens larger than his neighbors' or why he took long drives in the fall to find lanes without street signs. He would never know that he could inherit three hundred acres. But I couldn't bring myself to ask Stanley where she had gone.

Stanley arrived each morning fifteen minutes after my walk, a routine we'd started shortly after Mattie left. The first time I rang the dinner bell, Stanley arrived at my side door in minutes, as if he'd been waiting for the invitation. After that first morning, he didn't wait for the bell or even knock before entering. He brought his thermos and filled it with half the pot of coffee while I scrambled eggs and cut slices of bacon into the skillet. As he drank his first cup of coffee, I scooped two teaspoons of brown sugar into our oatmeal.

I could have asked him to wash the dishes or to take off his muddy boots before coming into the house, but cleaning at night became a way to fill my time. Every evening I wiped the rung that he propped his leg on when he balanced his plate on his knee. Outoors when he used his knee as a table, he appeared relaxed, but indoors it reminded me how long he had lived alone. And asking him to remove his muddy boots to walk around my house in sock feet seemed too intimate a request.

As I swept the floor each night, I realized how easily Stanley could fill the silence of this house. I often thought of the night we dug out the pipe and wondered what would have happened if I had stepped toward him and asked him to hold me. I considered inviting him for supper again, when we didn't have the excuse of work to rush us through our meal and leave the house quickly. But some nights when I walked through the empty upstairs, I wondered if I would want him to leave.

The past few Saturdays, Stanley joined the local boys at Jake's Diner on Route 42, where they spent three hours talking about work rather than working. At Jake's no one ever drank cold coffee. Jake's wife circled the fifteen-table restaurant with a steaming pot and topped off mugs before patrons drank a quarter of their cup of coffee. Everyone left behind a full cup of coffee, which some called wasteful and others called service. Once I went to the diner, shortly after my father's funeral, and they had added an extra coffee mug and set of silverware to the round table in the back corner. But after one Saturday, I knew I could not spend half a day with men who would only see me as farming my father's land. They dismissed every idea I had proposed that day for keeping soil worth farming on the sides of our valley.

Stanley came back from his Saturdays at Jake's smelling of stale grease and cigarette smoke. He told me their talk drifted to planting and then to Jim Yates's widow and the land she would now have to rent with no husband to plant it. From Stanley's offhand mention of this, I learned that Evelyn had returned from staying with her cousin in Mansfield. There was a chance she knew where Mattie had gone.

The edge of Evelyn Yates's woods looked no different than mine. Come winter our scrap piles were no longer hidden by May apples and touch-me-nots. Protruding from the snow, like bones, were rusted bicycle wheels, a washbasin, an old wagon bed, and other scraps that someone had once hoped to salvage. Her late husband had parked his 1951 Studebaker in the barn one afternoon, telling me his intention of reworking the engine when he found time. That was eight years ago. As I drove up next to the barn, one of his hunting dogs jumped out the open window of the front seat and the other crawled out the broken side door of the backseat. Had it not been for his dogs, it would have been fitting to bury that car in the plot next to Jim to hide his unfinished business. A new fear settled on me as I thought of the farmers of this valley who had died. I feared dying as my father had at my age in the middle of planting. The fields half-sown would serve as a daily reminder to anyone who drove past my farm that I had no heir.

The dogs' short, choked barks came in quick succession until one merely echoed the other. The heftier Brittany spaniel nudged my ankles while the smaller one pawed at my knees, a coordinated effort to dislodge the carrot cake that I clutched with both hands. I spent the afternoon looking for my mother's cream cheese icing recipe in a kitchen drawer filled with her batter-stained recipe cards. Even if I baked this cake every year, I could not remember the ratio of powdered sugar to milk. I finally found her recipe labeled "Never Fail Icing."

I yelled for Evelyn to call her dogs and nudged them to make a space for my next step. They pressed against my legs and barked for the only cake I enjoyed baking. Evelyn and I would talk for a good fifteen minutes about my mother's cream cheese icing; Evelyn seemed to prefer warming up to conversations with me by repeating our past conversations. She would ask if I managed to try my mother's icing on zucchini cake or cranberry cake, as she always asked when I brought this cake to her Christmas cookie exchange. We talked every year about the icing rather than the fact that I was the only woman in the valley who couldn't find the time to bake cookies. I didn't have the patience for dropping spoonfuls of dough onto cookie sheets when I could simply scoop cake batter into a pan. This past Christmas, Evelyn had not left her cousin's in Mansfield even for the cookie exchange.

The Hilliards' truck in the driveway shouldn't have surprised me. Evelyn opened the door, but Retha Hilliard invited me in and held the cake as I draped my coat over the dark walnut stair rail that Jim had carved for Evelyn as a wedding present. The house was chilled from months without heat. Evelyn wore a gray scarf and matching knitted hat, as if she didn't plan to stay, and Retha wore her yellow scarf wrapped around a navy turtleneck. Evelyn acted like a quiet visitor in her own home. Retha, who had fed the dogs for six months and kept an eye on the place, seemed comfortable in this house without Evelyn's husband in it. Evelyn watched Retha as if searching for a way to walk through this house without Jim.

Thanking me for the cake, Evelyn carried it into her dining room. It would have looked like Christmas had Evelyn covered her table with her plastic poinsettia tablecloth. The table held plates of sugar cookies, peanut butter buckeyes, and Ritz cracker tins filled with fudge. We responded to death with the same cookies and peanut brittle that we baked for the Christmas cookie exchange. Death and Christmas reminded us we shared something in common.

Retha came into the dining room and handed me a small plate. "Be a good neighbor and eat something." She held her smile too long. It was the smile of exhaustion.

"She's not doing well," Retha whispered as soon as Evelyn left the room. "Eat some cookies."

Retha was aging. An inch of gray feathered into her black hair, a deep black that could only come from a bottle. I tucked a short curl behind my ear as if I stood in front of the mirror. It had been six months since Mattie brought home a bottle of Lady Clairol and set out the hand towel, the plastic gloves, and the egg timer. Without Mattie to squirt the bottle and brush rivulets of brown from my forehead, I could not see coloring my hair.

Retha followed Evelyn into the kitchen where steam hissed from a teapot close to boiling. I had a taste for my mother's cream cheese icing from licking the spoon, but it seemed rude to slice my own cake. As I joined them, I nibbled on an oatmeal cookie, which had the stale taste of someone else's kitchen.

Evelyn decorated her kitchen with nostalgia. Framed 1920s advertisements hung in neatly matching frames. The apron-wearing women held soapboxes like shields. Under one collage of prints, Evelyn had hung a washboard and her mother's aprons on a row of pegs.

Evelyn leaned against the counter, gripping a mug with both hands and holding it close to her chest. She did not even face Retha, who was describing the new yarn store she had discovered at the latest strip of stores on Park Avenue outside Mansfield. I poured some hot tea and stood near Evelyn, angling myself away from Retha to see what Evelyn stared at intently. She looked directly into Jim's office. The metal desk showed as much disorder as his fields. For thirty-odd years of farming, Jim refused to rotate his crops. He preferred praying and then planting, as if God cared where he planted his winter wheat. When the rows of green shoots were only a shadow across the fields, it caused me to wonder, for a moment, if Jim had really heard an answer. I wondered if Evelyn now prayed for her own answers.

Retha talked about the yarn store without a single nod or smile from us to encourage her to continue. Colors, they had colors, she told us. She found more colors in one corner of the new shop than our local shop stocked altogether. They had coral reef, country sunset, carnival, and tundra. They had colors named for flowers, food and herbs: carnation, oatmeal, and oregano.

I leaned toward Evelyn and whispered, "It's better than silence." She glanced at me, and then at Retha, who had not heard me. Evelyn nodded. I wanted to say more, to tell her I could imagine how she felt. She had rearranged her life to fit her husband inside of it, but now she felt small, less like herself with him gone. She couldn't fill in the space that he had taken up. It seemed she must feel this, if I felt that way with Mattie gone.

Retha sipped her tea, and when neither Evelyn nor I filled the silence, she said, "These cookies need to get into the freezer." She found aluminum foil and then directed us into the dining room where she set us to wrapping up stacks of cookies. After we handed the wrapped cookies to Retha, she stacked the packets on a cookie tray to take to the freezer in the basement.

I glanced at the clock. Only two more hours of daylight remained for me to disinfect the buckets that would hang on the maple taps, yet I stayed. I hoped that eventually the talk would turn to Evelyn's cousin and to her cousin's son and then to Mattie. I couldn't bring myself to ask outright if Evelyn had seen Mattie without stirring up their curiosity.

They talked instead about Alice. They talked about Alice's health as if they were responsible for returning to her with a diagnosis.

"She's too worn down," Evelyn said. "I think she's tiring herself out."

"It's those children. They breed diseases that take them out for a few days and take an adult out for weeks," Retha said.

"She's substitute-teaching Home Economics," Evelyn said to me. Her overt politeness in including me only reminded us all that I rarely spent an afternoon with them.

"They let people as cranky as her with children?" I laughed at the thought of Alice teaching young women how to skimp on sugar when baking pies.

"Why? Are you interested in the job?" Retha smiled. At this Evelyn let out a short giggle. I liked seeing her smile. I handed her a stack of wrapped cookies.

"Mothers couldn't sign up their daughters fast enough if they found out I was teaching Home Ec," I said, causing them to laugh more.

"Alice tells me the woman she substitutes for wants to teach sex education," Evelyn said.

"That's not the place for it." Retha shook her head.

"Might be good for some girls," I said, hoping to turn their thoughts toward Mattie.

"Alice needs to quit working at the school," Evelyn said. "She won't help her husband by bringing home colds."

"It's better than selling off their land," Retha said.

"Is her husband that bad off?" I asked.

"Not as bad off as my father-in-law," Retha said. "He thinks you've run off with Morris," Retha said, as she ripped off sheets of foil and passed them to Evelyn and me. "He heard that Mattie left, and he got it in his head that you abandoned the farm."

It seemed she wanted me to laugh, but I could only ask, "He's that bad off? I'll get some fire in his veins and tell him Morris can't even plant a straight row of beans."

At this Evelyn surprised me by laughing. When I asked what was so funny about that, Retha explained for her, "That's what you and Morris would have spent your whole lives arguing about, how he couldn't farm your land as well as you could."

Evelyn glanced at Retha. She ripped more sheets of foil as if trying to cover the echoes of past conversations about me. In the twenty-five years since Morris returned home married to Charlotte, I knew they invented reasons for why he had left me. After twenty-five years, it surprised me they still remembered them. But we collected stories in this valley like we did old bicycles or moldboard plows, because they might have a use one day.

"All I'm saying is that Morris isn't a farmer," Evelyn said, as she glared at Retha. My chest tightened. I felt more isolated than if they talked about me to my face. She sighed. "I'm just saying he looks better in a suit than he ever did in overalls."

"That's the truth," Retha said. "He can fill out the shoulders of a suit."

"The way you're going on, maybe one of you should have married him."

The clock bell in the foyer reminded me that I had spent too much time with these women. It sounded the fourth ring, and I worried that I would have no daylight if I lingered. I crimped the foil around another stack of fudge and planned to leave when Evelyn said, "He was always yours, Dottie." Retha nodded.

Evelyn filled her own awkward silence by telling me how she watched us leave the school dance, how we seemed older than the students who stayed with the chaperones as they were told. When Evelyn embarrassed herself, she talked more. It seemed she had saved up every memory of Morris and me for this moment. She even remembered the wedding announcement, the first to come out of our class. Then she told me what I had come to find out. Remembering the wedding I never had seemed to bring to mind other weddings. "Even at Mattie's wedding, it still surprised me to see Morris with Charlotte," she said. "Of course, I hardly saw him after he moved, and before that I only saw him with you."

So Mattie had married. In all those weeks that I walked my land thinking of her return, she had married a way out of this town.

"Were you both at the wedding?" I asked. They did not seem to realize that I did not know about it. Retha shook her head. "No, they kept it small."

"Family only," Evelyn said. "They married at Morris's house. My cousin's house is only half the size, and besides, it seemed more appropriate at the bride's family than the groom's. My cousin baked the cake, and I made my sherbet punch."

I nodded rather than flinch at the mention of the bride's family. I pitied Mattie in a small apartment, keeping house for a young boy with dreams larger than the love he would have for Mattie and a baby.

In marrying, Mattie had already settled. She had not even managed to have the wedding she had planned, the one she described at the age of twelve after she told me she forgot Zela's face. I had shown her my only picture of Zela, her wedding photograph, in her parents' living room on an October afternoon. In the picture she stood alone where they had married in front of the fireplace, smiling demurely, too much like a bride. Her straight dress had an empire waist and a bit of lace around the square neckline. Zela turned her hand in the photograph to show the round half-carat diamond that she wore over her white glove. The wedding ring I kept in a velvet ring box in my nightstand, but I had not mentioned this to Mattie when I showed her the photograph, and now I was glad.

Mattie had taken my only picture of Zela from my office when she left. But taking that picture had not reminded her of the wedding she wanted. She told me she would marry in a church, and the church bells would ring for a half hour after they walked down the aisle. She wanted a train longer than her mother's. I never asked her why she wanted a wedding different from her mother's.

"How did Mattie look?" I asked.

"There's no need to be ashamed of her. Her dress hid everything."

I did not correct her, but I did not know how to ask again. I wanted to know if Mattie looked happy. So I said instead, "It didn't hide her well enough for you to forget." Retha and Evelyn glanced at one another. Later when they talked about me, they would remember my words as being harsher than I intended them.

"Well at least they married," Retha replied.

"And that will solve everything?" I asked.

"It's admirable to see a young man take responsibility these days. Seems so many want to dodge every duty. Our men acted like men," Evelyn said.

"There's nothing admirable about doing the right thing after you do the wrong thing," I said. "He could have saved himself a lot of trouble."

"Give the boy credit," Retha said. "He could have abandoned Mattie and left them to live with you."

Rather than admitting I wished he had, I said, "We would have managed." They would never understand that Mattie's child would not know his way home. "I hope he married her because he loved her."

Evelyn smiled as if I said something right. She patted my hand. "A boy doesn't leave California to work in a steel mill if he doesn't love a girl."

"The steel mill was hiring?" I asked, trying to understand.

"My cousin's husband got him the job that he's held for him since he first taught him to weld."

"Evelyn, you have enough baked goods here to open a small bakery," I said cheerfully. I wanted to hug them both and sit down for a slice of cake and a cup of coffee, even though the afternoon had slipped past me. We had worked into darkness, none of us noticing when the soft gray winter sky had hardened into night. I flipped the light switch behind me. Each of us blinked rapidly, prompting laughter that made the room warmer. I smiled at them and offered to help Retha carry the cookies to the freezer in the basement.

"Please, you two take some of this home with you," Evelyn said, shoving stacks of cookies toward us. No one had even uncovered my cake. I waited until Retha took a few small stacks of cookies. I slipped on my coat and gloves, picked up my carrot cake, and told Evelyn to call if she needed anything. Stanley would not turn down a slice of cake, and then I would tell him I had a plan to bring Mattie home.

Chapter Twenty

When I drove home from Evelyn's, it was dark enough for high beams and too early for neighbors to close their drapes. Rectangles of light streamed from kitchens where wives moved purposefully at their work. The light snow on the fields would soon sparkle with moonlight, but at this hour the woods were darker than night and the fields appeared gray in comparison. My breath fogged the wide windshield of my truck until its navy hood was indistinguishable from the dark road. A few yards beyond Zela's old farm, I pulled to the side of the road to scrape the inside of the windshield with my driver's license. A single light shone in the front window of the old farmhouse. I glanced in the rearview mirror and then drove in reverse until I parked the truck near the lane that led to the brick house.

The old woman who lived there kept a small Tiffany lamp lit on a table flush with the front window. Every evening she turned on the lamp; it suggested a hospitality she never demonstrated otherwise. No one visited this farm other than the men who rented and farmed her five hundred acres. Morris sold this land to his father's cousin who was a Brubaker in name, but not in ability. He only managed to farm for ten years before he died, willing the most respected farm in the valley to his wife who turned down every offer for the land. This was what happened to land without heirs.

I cut off my headlights. At this hour, in this darkness, no one would notice my pickup outside the two-story house that had once been the envy of the valley. This house had inspired men to settle on this land and encouraged their wives to agree to it. Ten years later I still thought of Zela in my sitting room every time I looked at her old house. I often slowed as I drove past, hoping at different hours of the day that I might see what she had seen. Sometimes I wondered if the sight of the house in daylight would have caused her to pack Mattie back in the car and drive home without the gasoline.

Had it been daylight she would have seen that the mortar had crumbled, exposing the edges of the bricks to be chipped by rain and wind. The gray window casings looked white only at dusk. She might have seen why she left the valley in the first place and remembered that she wanted to raise her daughter on doctors' row. This was something I never discussed with Mattie. I had to believe Zela was drawn back to this valley because she realized we had been born to work this land and for the land to work its way in us. This was what Mattie needed to understand. Her child belonged here as much as she did.

The plan to bring Mattie home had come to me fully formed. Stanley and I would build them a house at the edge of the farm, a house larger than any apartment they could afford in Mansfield. Travis would drive the thirty minutes to the steel mill every day, but soon he would hate the drive and working for his father and eventually ask to work on the farm instead.

As I looked at Zela's old house, I knew why the widow kept the small lamp lit. It was the same reason I left the kitchen light on when I went into the living room. Before Mattie it would have been wasteful to leave lights on in an empty room; now it seemed necessary. But tonight I would invite Stanley to share the carrot cake with me, and I would only need the light on in the living room. A single lit room would not seem as lonely with another person in the house.

I clicked on my headlights and eased the truck from the gravel berm back onto the road. Before I went to Stanley's, I would brew coffee. Of course he would be finishing up his supper at this hour, which would leave me enough time to build a fire and set out the cake in the living room. As we ate we would sketch the house and list the materials. Then we would set our plates and cups aside. For a moment I imagined the warmth of leaning into Stanley and the comfort of him pulling me toward him. It had been so long since I had been with Morris I could hardly remember the feel of a man near me, but I wanted it just the same.

It was foolishness to think on this any longer. I drove down the lane directly to Stanley's. There was no reason he couldn't build the fire while I got out the graph paper for the drawings and materials list. Yet as I drove toward his place, I decided to let him choose what time he left my house that night.

The uneaten carrot cake lay at the bottom of the trash can. The night before I had tossed it as soon as I entered the house alone. Then I had crawled into bed fully clothed under extra blankets pungent with the smell of Mattie's lavender-scented soap that I also stored in the linen closet. I had not bothered with supper, which was why I woke at four the next morning hungry. I wanted a basket of warm biscuits, and I wanted to sit in bed and eat one after the other until my stomach was so heavy with them I could sleep through the day. But as I stirred the dough and spooned it onto a baking sheet, I decided Mattie and Travis would need a place to stay before we finished the house.

By seven o'clock I had stripped my parents' room of all of its linens. First I folded the sheets that covered their furniture and dropped them into a laundry basket to wash on Tuesday with the other towels and sheets. I rolled the quilt and tied twine around it to store in the attic. The open window let in a breeze that carried away the dust and the faintest scent of the rose water that my mother dotted on her wrists and neck. I knew the room could not still hold her smell, but I smelled it just the same.

The door of the bedroom slammed shut from a gust of wind, and the room filled with air chilled from blowing across snow-covered fields. After I took down the heavy lace curtains, I noticed the wallpaper. My mother brought the wallpaper with her from Erie. For years she complained that if she had known she could never afford to wallpaper another room, she would not have wasted it on a room that visitors never saw.

Moistened by the steam of humid summers, some strips had separated from the glue and curled away from the top of the wall. This paper would never suit Mattie, so I ripped off the sections I could reach, tugging long strips until they tore near the ceiling. I should have gone to the barn for the stepladder, but I did not want to face Stanley this morning. He would never know my hopes for last evening, but I feared my face would betray my disappointment.

Even through the closed door, I heard Stanley come into the kitchen. Hoping he would look for me in the machine shed, I stood still with a sheet of wallpaper in my hands. I turned away when he came up the stairs and let himself into the room.

"Most people knock before opening a closed bedroom door," I said and tugged on a strip that tore before I lifted my arms above my shoulder. It would take hours to finish this job right.

"What else would you be doing at this hour but working?"

"What if I had brought a man home with me last night?"

Stanley chuckled as if I told a joke. "If you had a man here, you wouldn't have breakfast dishes washed and drying. And the kitchen smells like coffee, but there's none left."

"I poured it out. Didn't see any reason to leave it in the pot." Crumpling the wad of paper, I tossed it in the pile near his feet. He smiled as if we were enjoying this conversation. My throat closed with anger. I could hardly breathe with him in the room.

"I'll make enough for both of us, and when it's ready you can have another cup with me," he said.

"Is that how this works? You come into my kitchen and help yourself to coffee?" The words felt forced. I couldn't forget the night before. The shades of his house were drawn, and the waitress's green Pinto sat outside his house. Cutting my headlights, I saw their shadows at his kitchen table, not across from one another as friends but sitting with their chairs close together near the corner of the table. I went to bed not wanting to hear what time she left.

"It didn't bother you yesterday to share your coffee or eggs," he said.

I scooped up an armful of wallpaper shreds and walked past him. "You've got it pretty good. Drinking hot coffee for the first hour of your day's work."

He followed me downstairs as I shoved the wallpaper into the trash can. While I brewed coffee, Stanley took our two mugs from the dish drainer from the morning before.

"Stop waking early. It makes you grouchy," he said.

I smiled now, because I needed his help. I took out the graph paper and motioned for him to sit beside me at the table. "I have a new project for you."

He stood with an empty mug in hand waiting for the coffee. "Good morning, Stanley. Good morning, Dottie," he said with forced politeness. "Maybe we start the morning with coffee before you start bossing me."

Rather than remind him I was his boss, I nodded. "Did you want some eggs with that coffee?"

"Would be nice," he said warily. He sat at the table with his hands circling his empty coffee mug. As I whisked the eggs, he watched me. I pooled a tablespoon of oil in the pan and scrambled the eggs. "Who made you angry?" he asked. "The women did not like your cake?"

I sprinkled pepper over the eggs the way he liked it and scooped the steaming eggs onto his plate. "It's the Never Fail Icing. I could put it on a hamburger bun, and they'd tell me they'd never eaten a better cake."

I sat across from him as he sliced his fork and knife across the eggs the way he did with anything I set in front of him. After Mattie first left, his habits kept me from thinking of her. He filled my mornings with thoughts of what my life could be like with a man as a part of it. This morning though, I realized I had not merely thought of sharing my life with any man. I had allowed myself to imagine a life with Stanley.

"Do you have enough coffee in your belly to hear about this project?"

He said little as I sketched out my plan. I drew a house with three rooms bigger than the house he had built for himself nearly eight years ago. It would be one story with a small foyer and a ten-by-ten front room. The kitchen would be large enough for a table, and the two bedrooms would face the hill so the morning sun would not wake the baby. If Stanley was pleased that I thought of a way to bring Mattie back to us, he did not show it. When I could not take his silence another minute, I finally asked, "Don't you want Mattie nearby?"

He shrugged as if I spoke of a neighbor girl whom he had never met.

"You think it's too much work," I said.

"Travis will have a long drive."

"How long have you known she stayed in Mansfield?"

"You never looked for her, never asked. Why would you want to know where she lived?"

He talked as if his words were not meant to hurt me. He touched a finger to the bits of egg on the plate and licked it off.

"I said I wouldn't run after her. That doesn't mean I didn't care what happened to her."

He stood and took his plate to the sink. As he rinsed it, he said quietly, "She seems happy where she is. You will only make yourself more angry if she says no."

I examined the sketch of the house and with a few quick erasures of walls and quick lines I enlarged the kitchen and added a larger closet onto Mattie's room. I drew another window in the living room to overlook the bottom field and add more light, even though it would only increase the cost.

Stanley refilled his coffee and motioned for mine. The growing tightness in my chest and neck made it difficult to even shake my head. He seemed only capable of hurting me with his words this morning. As he sat at the table, he turned the sketch toward him to study it.

"She is settled in their apartment."

"So are you saying you won't help? I can't build this without you."

"If Mattie and Travis want the house, I will help build it."

"If the girl has any sense, she'll realize that if she moves here she stands to inherit this farm."

Stanley drew his finger around the sketched rooms. He did not have the expression of a man figuring dimensions or planning materials to build this house. Instead, he stared at the paper as if to avoid looking at me.

"You hope only for things you can't have," he finally said.

"Why don't you tell me what you mean by that?"

He leaned closer to me, his breath warm on my face. "Mattie told me of a man you loved. A man you still love."

I drew back from him. "Mattie knows nothing about me. I stopped loving him the day he married someone else."

"You do not know your own heart."

"I know I haven't had time for love. I ran a farm and eased my parents' deaths. I raised a girl who was not mine."

He laid his hand over mine. "You are a proud woman. I said to myself, this woman is so hardheaded, if you ever convince her to love you, she will never stop."

The warmth of his hand spread through me as if I had eased my dusty, work-worn body into a hot bath. If he had not held my hand, his words would have passed so quickly I would not have heard them. I wished I could lean into him, but the corner of the table jutted awkwardly between us. Then I saw our reflection in the window. The two of us sat at the table as he had with the waitress the night before. I drew my hand from his.

"I will not be taken for a fool, Stanley. Don't look surprised. I saw that waitress's car at your house last night."

Stanley chuckled and leaned back in his chair until he looked at the ceiling. "Of course you do not ask me why she comes to my house. She's moving to New Mexico and wanted to sell her car. She offered it to me and tried to convince me to drive it to Florida to work in the citrus groves."

"Why would she want you in Florida?"

"So I could make something of myself. She says I stay here for the same wrong reasons that she stayed. But she woke up one morning and realized the married man she loved would always be married."

"So you're leaving," I said as a cold settled over me. He would follow this woman. I understood now why he had not wanted to look at the plans for the house.

"I told her that the woman I loved wasn't married, so it wasn't as easy to stop hoping."

"I know better than to trust a man who can speak love to two women."

Stanley shook his head. "I have been a foolish man. Love keeps no record of wrong. Yet you, Dottie, keep records so long they run together, and one man pays another man's debt."

He stood and cupped my chin in his hand. "Good-bye, Dottie," he said.

When I said nothing, he bowed his head as he had when we first met. He left quickly. The screen door banged and caught on the latch.

I forced myself to stand. I would go back to ripping off wallpaper, so I would not have to see a taxi pick him up. I would rip every last shred from the walls, so I would not be tempted to try to stop him from leaving.

Chapter Twenty-one

An oak tree could stand for two hundred years, withstanding fire, lightning, man, and blight. Long enough for eight generations to angle new houses and lanes to benefit from its shade. Long enough to hold tree houses and swings that would rot and fall from them like a slow autumn. Long enough to forget they could fall.

Years ago lightning had felled one of my oldest oaks, which had shaded my bedroom and kitchen from the morning sun. Even now when I glanced out the window, I looked first at the stump rather than at the expanse of field behind it. If I had planted a sapling the day after the tree fell, I would not live long enough for it to shade my bedroom. As I stared out the kitchen window at the weather-beaten stump, I realized that I would continue to look for Stanley walking across my farm for a long time to come.

These thoughts did not accomplish anything. I scraped out my bowl of half-eaten oatmeal into the trash. I could not waste time missing a man who cared so little for me that his half-finished projects littered the farm. A tractor was propped up in the machine shed waiting for a part. Sawed boards were stacked along the back wall of the barn to repair the floor in the spring. In the days after he left, I walked the farm with pencil and paper, taking note of the unfinished work. I had done the same the day after my father's funeral. If I slowed down, I would remember I missed them.

If I hoped to convince Mattie to return to the farm before the ground thawed, I had much to accomplish. With Stanley's house sitting empty, I would not need to build a new one by spring. The one-bedroom house would not look as cramped once it was clean, so I set off toward it with a wad of rags stuffed in my coat pocket, a bucket, and a bottle of vinegar.

Stanley was a neat man, but he did not know how to clean. He hung his hat on the same peg every evening when he came through the door, but he never washed the curtains that Mattie sewed for him in Home Economics in eighth grade. I swept crumbling carcasses of flies from the windowsills and scoured the bathtub until the porcelain shone. The sharp tang of vinegar drove out the last smells of Stanley.

The note that he pinned to the corkboard in the machine shed made it clear that he did not plan to return, and I did not want his soapy, warm scent lingering behind him. He claimed in the note that he would work in the orange groves in Florida and that the waitress still planned to move to New Mexico, but he doubted that I would believe him.

I washed down the rough log walls before scrubbing the wood plank floor. Stanley lived as though he expected a wife to wash field dust from the floors while he worked the land. It would not be difficult for him to find this sort of woman. But I couldn't shake the feeling that if he wanted a woman like this, he wouldn't have worked ten years for me.

I told myself that if Mattie had answered the telephone instead of Travis, things would have turned out differently. Even after I scrubbed out Stanley's house and washed and hung the curtains, it took me days to call Mattie. After only four months, she had become a stranger to me. Travis surprised me by answering the phone at two in the afternoon, but he explained he had switched to second shift at the steel mill. Flustered, I asked him if Mattie had delivered the baby.

"When did you decide to take an interest in our baby?"

I smiled at his urge to protect her. I felt more inclined to like him after imagining us working the farm together. "After I found out you didn't take the baby to California. How does Mattie feel?"

"Swollen. She's afraid her skin won't stretch another inch."

I laughed, relieved by his moment of friendliness. "Is she there?"

He paused long enough for me to think that he had handed the phone to Mattie. But then he cleared his throat as if to add consequence to his words. "Mattie doesn't want to talk to you."

"I see," I said, but I wasn't about to let her stubbornness keep her baby from growing up where Brubakers had raised generations. "I have a baby gift for you that might make your lives a little easier."

"That's kind of you."

"My hired man moved out, leaving me with an empty house. It's the right size for the three of you. You'd never have to pay a dime of rent. As your family grows, we'll build a bigger house."

I interpreted his sudden silence for gratitude until he asked, "So I should move my pregnant wife a half-hour from the hospital and drive to work when I can walk three blocks from here?"

I had imagined us sitting at the kitchen table eating a bowl of vegetable soup with crusty homemade wheat bread when I divulged my plans for leaving them the farm. At times I'd even imagined myself holding the sleeping baby. But I sensed his urge to hang up, so I said, "Between us, if you learn to work this farm, I plan to leave it to you and Mattie."

"You can't suddenly act like you care about her," Travis said quietly.

"Are you happy, Travis? In a half an hour, the whistle at the steel mill will call you indoors for eight hours. Is that what you want?"

"Every day we plan on how to leave this place, but nothing would convince Mattie to return to your farm."

I felt generous in my offer and hadn't prepared myself for this. How could they reject my forgiveness of Mattie for her cruelty in our last conversation? Travis sided with her without considering what he was turning down.

"Before you judge me, young man, remember that I took Mattie to raise even though I had a farm to run."

"You wouldn't have your farm without Mattie's inheritance."

I nearly told him he would not have Mattie for a wife if she had not wanted to leave my farm. But Travis's words hit like a fierce, cold wind. And I could not catch my breath.

He cleared his throat again. I believed he would spend years trying to feel old enough for the life he had mistakenly stepped into. "It would be best if you didn't call again," he said.

I slowly lowered the phone after Travis hung up. I stared out the window without knowing how long my hand rested on the phone. The wind blew the morning's snow from the pine trees stirring up a greater storm than when it gently fell in the early hours of the day. Without a plan, I wrapped my scarf around my neck and quickly buttoned up my jacket as if I had somewhere to go. I would not spend the afternoon alone in this house or on this farm.

After Stanley left, I avoided Pete's Hardware. The tractor in the shed only needed a belt, but shopping at Pete's meant facing people who would ask where Stanley went. I slowly opened the hardware store door, knowing it would ring the bell hanging on the inside of the door. Pete liked bells. Customers could summon him to the cash register with an antique register bell. Cowbells hung at the end of every aisle for customers to ring for assistance. Behind the counter was an old school bell that Pete rang to summon his two employees.

I could lose time here, walking through the aisles and reminding myself of new projects I could undertake.

Choosing an aisle empty of customers, I picked up a broad hatchet as if to judge its sharpness, but in truth I hoped the cool hard metal would keep my thoughts from returning to my conversation with Travis. By the time I reached the sockets and wrenches, I knew that even if Mattie had answered the phone she too would have refused me.

How could I have believed that she would move back to the farm when she would not even speak to me on the phone? She married without inviting me. She lived a half an hour from me for four months without contacting me. She had, in fact, become too much like me.

As I heard someone walking in the next aisle, I turned toward the display at the end of the aisle. I wanted to leave the store without talking to anyone.

"Are you anticipating a beetle problem come spring, Dottie?" Retha Hilliard's husband came up next to me. I noticed for the first time that I stood in front of a display of Levin insecticides. With his earflap hat covering his balding head, he looked more than ever like his father. He was almost as old as his father was when he first walked my fields with me.

"You never know, Howard." I smiled. "How's Retha?"

"She's at the new knitting store buying every color they have. She's on her third pair of slippers for my father."

"I bet he loses every pair."

Howard laughed and then frowned as if I had said something wrong. "It's hard for him to lose things when everything is labeled Hilliard in permanent marker."

"Do you have a problem with your boys stealing the old man's underwear?"

Howard shook his head. "We put him in Longview Nursing Home last week. Retha didn't want to tell you."

"Is that so?"

"She's worried you'll make it worse by commiserating with him. It's been hard enough as it is."

It was clear from his hunched shoulders and his hands driven into his pockets, like a small child trying to fold in on himself, that Retha had made the decision. It would not help Howard to tell him that his father should die walking his fields in work boots, rather than walking the halls of a nursing home in knitted slippers, so I said, "I heard my Uncle Charlie ended up there before he died, and he had the money to choose the best."

"From what I heard, he had your money to choose the best."

"So that's what you heard."

"You know, my father said Charlie was so crooked they'd have to screw him into the ground when he died."

I laughed. "And that's why I love your father. I can't imagine that he's happy with his new arrangement."

"He's furious. He speaks to me, but he won't talk to me."

"I might have to visit him and do some commiserating."

Howard laughed and then worked his wallet out of his back pocket. "I want you to take something to him."

I left the hardware store with a flannel shirt, jeans, and instructions from Howard to convince his father that he looked ridiculous wearing a nightshirt all hours of the day.

Had Mr. Hilliard looked in any condition to escape, I would have hoisted him up to the window and crawled out after him. On the drive to Mansfield, I'd considered fixing up my parents' room for him. Before I saw him, it seemed reasonable that he could sit in my living room as easily as he could sit in a recreation room in Mansfield. But he wasn't sitting. He lay on his back with one hand atop the other as if preparing to be lifted into a casket.

The same gray linoleum floors in the lobby extended into each of the rooms as if to remind the residents they were not trusted on carpet. The room had a single window that only those standing could see out of, but the closed, stale air of the room suggested it had never been opened. His roommate dozed in a wheelchair holding his false teeth in his lap.

I pulled the curtain between the beds trying to wake him. I hoped when he woke I would feel less embarrassed for him. His nightshirt was buttoned lower than any of his work shirts, revealing his chest, a painful white that had never seen the July sun. He did not have the even tan of his grandson, who rolled and wrapped his undershirt around his head in June and worked outdoors bare-chested until September. Mr. Hilliard opened his eyes for a moment and then closed them.

"Did you come to stare at me or talk to me?" he asked without opening his eyes.

"I don't usually talk to people who look too tired to roll over."

"I wasn't sleeping. Would you keep your eyes open in this place?"

"Your roommate seems entertaining."

He chuckled and watched me as I settled in my chair holding the flannel shirt. With his eyes open, he did not look as frail. "Only at night," he said. "He thinks his wife is in my bed."

"What do you tell him?"

"Nothing. It keeps his blood flowing. The nurse said he's improved now that I'm here."

I shook out the shirt and told him I'd brought him something decent to wear. He leaned his pillow against the wall and pushed himself upright. Wisps of hair stuck out in all directions from the back of his head from lying too long in one position. He fingered the sleeve as if assessing its quality and then slipped it on over his nightshirt. The stiff, unwashed collar made him look sturdier. He said nothing as he smoothed the arms and buttoned the sleeves tight around his wrists. I had never seen him in a flannel shirt that had not faded on the clothesline. He looked confident and small, like a caricature of a farmer.

"Are you still trying to get corn out of those sorry excuses for fields?"

I settled into my chair. Here was someone I could talk to.

"Do you want me to get you out of here?" I asked.

"I prefer strange women giving me my baths." He smiled.

I laughed, though it saddened me that he knew he had to stay here. "Don't rely on Retha to tell me what you need. You know to call me."

"There's nothing that woman can't knit for me. Don't worry about me."

He settled back into his pillow and closed his eyes. I waited a few minutes and then stood quietly. He opened his eyes with an alertness that surprised me.

"Can't a man rest his eyes without you thinking he's sleeping?"

"I'll come back later if you're tired."

"You're the first person today who hasn't asked me if I've had a bowel movement. Don't be too quick to leave."

I sat near him and leaned toward the bed. "Tell me something then," I said. "Which of your grandsons would you trust to run my farm?"

"I know you miss me, but you're too young to check in here."

"I'm not planning on leaving my farm anytime soon. I thought one of your boys could start working with me now with a promise to inherit the farm. I'd rather leave it to one of them than let the state have it."

"What about that girl of yours?"

"You mean Zela's girl?" I corrected him.

"I know who I'm talking about. Why wouldn't you leave it to her?"

"She'd chop it into five-acre lots and sell it to the highest bidder."

"When you're gone, you're gone. You can't run it from the grave, though I knew men who tried. My father-in-law left instructions in his will so detailed he might as well have told me I couldn't farm."

"I haven't worked my entire life to improve the soil so Mansfielders can buy my land and have bountiful backyard gardens. You can't tell me you would want that."

"I'm saying I'll never know. There comes a point when a man has to believe his life was worth living while he was living it. I can't spend the end of my life hoping that everyone else lives the way I want him to once I'm gone."

"It's easier to feel that way when you have a son and three grandsons working your land just as you taught them."

"Maybe," he admitted. "If you need one of my boy's help, you don't have to dangle the farm in front of him. I'll talk to Howard about it. Your hired man probably isn't looking as spry as he did when you first hired him."

"The fact is I don't have a hired man. He left a few weeks ago."

"I thought you'd finally found one you wouldn't run off."

"He ran off on his own. He believed a woman who told him he could make more money in citrus groves in Florida."

"I'd start wondering if I were you," he said.

"Wondering what?"

"Why I couldn't keep another soul on that farm with me."

"I suppose I work them too hard."

"Could be. Could be," he said with little certainty.

A nurse opened up the curtain between the residents and wheeled a medicine cart next to Mr. Hilliard's bed. She handed him a glass of chocolate milk with a straw bobbing in it as if he was a child who would dribble the milk down his chin. He opened his hand to show her he swallowed the pills and took two sips of milk before handing back the glass. As soon as she walked out of the room, he spit the pills into his hand.

"They make my head as jiggly as Jell-O," he said. "Don't be telling Retha."

I handed him a tissue, and after he wiped his hand, I tossed the pills in his roommate's trash.

By the time I arrived home, it was too late to wait for the leftover stew to warm on the stove. I lathered two pieces of bread with peanut butter and, between them, sliced butter and a banana. This was my father's snack, and tonight I wanted simple comfort. For the entire drive home, Mr. Hilliard's words worked on me like a pebble in my boot.

I took the sandwich and a glass of milk into my office. It was Thursday, and I had bills to pay. On Thursdays I often remembered Mattie's words that when I died I would shake my fist at God for interrupting my schedule.

I took my record book from the shelf above my desk and flicked on the printing calculator. The soft whir caused me to hear the steady tick of the kitchen clock, the only other sound in the house. Record books lined the shelf above me: a book for each year, a different color for each decade. Navy for the forties, black for the fifties, burgundy for the sixties, gray for the seventies: the solid colors absorbed light and gave gravity to the task. Where my father had faltered in maintaining records, I had succeeded. Even though Charlie had died five years earlier, I kept every one of his receipts stapled in the books to prove, if needed, that I paid more for my farm than it could ever be worth.

I unlocked the safe under my desk where I kept the ring binder of business checks with five to a page. This routine still brought me pleasure. In this office, I saw my efforts translated into numbers. After I recorded the amount on the stubs to the side of the checks, I figured the debits and credits on the printing calculator, sharpened a pencil over the trash can, and then meticulously copied the numbers into the record book. I stapled the tape to the page in case I needed to trace back and find an error.

I wished I could trace back to what caused each person to leave this farm. Then I could prove to Mr. Hilliard that they had left for their own reasons, not just because of me. I turned to the back of the record book and wrote on the back page *A Record of Their Leaving*. Morris had married Charlotte. Mattie had married Travis. If Stanley had gone to New Mexico with the waitress, it would have made the list simple. But these reasons were too simple to be true; they ignored what came before their leaving. Still, it pinched at my heel to have Mr. Hilliard suggest that I had driven the three of them from this farm. The fact remained, though, that I was alone and had never allowed myself to consider why.

But no one plowed over the same rock twice. You removed it or you risked destroying your equipment. I never pondered why a rock blocked my path. I dug it up and buried it in land I never intended to farm. When Morris left me, I tried to remove him from my thoughts and continue on.

My father taught me that labor was the appropriate response to grief, that sorrow and loneliness were fruitless emotions that would not give me the strength to press into the day and work to exhaustion. These emotions would not yield anything I could point to and be proud of. Work had kept me from looking over my shoulder for Morris or Stanley to return. But Stanley's accusations stayed with me. Had I expected him to right Morris's wrongs?

This list of their leaving told me nothing. I closed the record book and slid it next to the other gray books on the shelf above my desk. The history of this farm could be read in these numbers. Running my hand along the books, I counted back ten years and took a burgundy book from the shelf.

I flipped through the book looking for the two-line transaction. On a Thursday in March, I credited and debited three hundred thousand dollars. In a single line, I spent every dollar that Zela left to Mattie. I had written "From Mattie Morgan" and "To Rex Connell." These two lines told a truth I ignored for ten years.

Beneath this entry, the columns of numbers continued uninterrupted in neat rows. No entries separated these two transactions. I had not hesitated in the brief moments between collecting and spending Mattie's money. Had I even thought of her?

Rummaging through my top desk drawer, I found a black marker and a ruler. With the same precision that I first used to record these numbers, I darkened the preprinted line between Mattie and Rex's names. I wrote at the end of the line *My Record of Wrongs*. For every reason I had raised her, not a single one had been for her.

My stomach contracted with sadness, and I wrapped my arms around myself. The silence of the room draped me like a damp quilt. I wanted to speak into the emptiness of the room.

"Mattie," I said.

I had the urge to pray aloud. It brought an unexpected comfort to think of prayer, and for a moment, the room did not feel as empty. I did not feel alone.

Yet praying for weather while I walked my fields was one matter. I simply added my voice to the murmur of prayers rising up from our valley. Praying out loud in the house was entirely different. Why would God regard a solitary prayer from someone who avoided Him more than believed in Him?

But on this night, I spoke into the silence. Without closing my eyes or kneeling as my mother taught me, I said, "I've made a mess of things. I'm sorry." It hardly seemed like a prayer, but it was the most honest thing I had ever spoken.

Chapter Twenty-two

Occasionally in the *Mansfield Journal,* Morris's picture appeared with the Rotary Club or the VFW's annual chili cook-off; so on the day he visited me, the thirty pounds he had gained came as no surprise. What startled me was his visit. That Sunday afternoon I was settled in front of the fire reading the newspaper when he rang the doorbell at the front door. As I tugged on the door still stubborn with disuse, dread dropped into my stomach, and I thought only of Mattie.

A week earlier I had sent a letter to Morris asking him to write when Mattie had her baby. My worry for her shadowed my work. Zela had not fared well in childbirth; she had been too tired to feed or even hold Mattie. Her labor had been long and damaging, leaving a barren womb. Still hoping for children, I had not understood why Zela said it was for the best she had only one child. Now I understood that, even then, Zela wanted to tell me about Nathaniel. What else had she tried to say about her marriage? What had she tried to tell me by naming me in her will? Whatever it was, I had betrayed her and, in the end, betrayed Mattie. I would not call and apologize to Mattie, because it could not fix what I had done, so I had written Morris.

As he stomped the snow from his boots, he assured me Mattie was fine. I invited him in and took his snow-covered coat as he complained of the unusual snowfall for April. Larger than any Brubaker I'd ever known, he carried his weight low along his waistline and in his shoulders and chest. It was where powerful men gained weight, not slothful ones. He dusted the snow from a new beard that he had grown, presumably, to hide the softening of his jaw line. He had not been to the farm since Mattie turned sixteen, when she borrowed my truck to visit them. He had not come into the house after I decided to keep Mattie.

Remembering he disliked reheated coffee, I offered to brew a fresh pot. As we waited for the coffee, we talked more of the weather and the changes Morris saw driving into the valley. A field his father had farmed was overgrown with leafless saplings of maple and beech. He did not seem as troubled by this as I wanted him to be. Everything we said merely covered a silence that rose up in long, awkward pauses.

Morris settled into one corner of the couch and I in the other with the middle cushion definitively between us. Morris wore a green wool sweater, jeans, and heavy off-white wool socks. He had kicked off his snow boots at the door, and his stocking feet made him seem comfortably at home. These details thrust themselves on me, and I adjusted to the shift in my quiet

Sunday afternoon. I relaxed near him, my muscles remembering comfort in his presence.

Mattie's baby came early, and he was now a week old. "I thought you should know," he said as his only explanation for driving a half an hour to give me this news.

"Is Mattie okay?"

"Her labor lasted thirty-six hours."

"Did you tell her Zela's was forty-two?"

"I'd forgotten that."

"So she had a son?"

Morris nodded with a smile. I could not envision Mattie with a baby any more than I could imagine her with Travis before I met him. I said, "To think Zela would have been a grandmother. I still have trouble believing she's the only one of us who had a child."

Morris cleared his throat and shifted uncomfortably in his corner of the couch. I recognized in his sudden glance at his feet that he thought I meant to hurt him, so I said, "I'm sure he'll bring you a lot of joy."

"He already has. Charlotte practically lives in their tiny apartment. She's filled their freezer with meals they don't eat because she cooks dinner every night."

His words could have easily cut into me. Charlotte had what I had wanted. But she had not purposefully kept Morris from me as I had kept Mattie from her.

"It will be hard for you and Charlotte if they move to California," I said.

"Even with Travis working overtime, they won't leave anytime soon. If they settle there, Charlotte's already planned for us to retire there."

We both stared into the crumbling fire as an awkwardness settled between us. Neither of us had finished our coffee. I picked at a stray string on the cording of the floral couch. Morris crossed his feet as if deciding to stay and then uncrossed them as if deciding to leave.

"You could have called or mailed a note," I said.

"I know," he said, "but Travis told me your hired man left, and you were alone."

Though I had avoided anger only moments earlier, the old fury pierced me, like the sharp corner of my dresser catching me in the side in the dark. I steadied my voice and said evenly, "Don't think you need to pity me. Why would you suddenly care that I'm alone?"

Morris sighed and stroked his beard, as if he had always gathered his thoughts this way. "It's been over twenty-five years, Dottie. What do you want from me?"

"Our engagement ended without a single word."

"What can we have to say now?"

I was too angry to consider this a reasonable question. He had seemingly gone on with his life for twenty-five years without a thought of me. I still wanted to know why. "Did you know I came to the train station the day you returned?"

"This won't solve anything. You're determined to hate me." Morris set his coffee cup on the pile of magazines on the end table. He leaned forward on the couch preparing to stand.

"I came to the train station to surprise you," I said. "You turned to help Charlotte off the train or else you would have seen me. I spent the three-hour bus ride home wondering what I had done wrong. Why you hadn't at least broken our engagement."

Morris looked toward the fire. His cheek twitched, and he sighed as he leaned back onto the couch. "When I married Charlotte, I couldn't explain to myself what I had done. All I knew was that I liked myself better with her."

What had I expected from his answer? All these years I had wanted to ask why, not because I wanted to know, but because I wanted him to know how much he had hurt me.

My silence prompted Morris to fill it. "After you kept Mattie, I wondered how I ever loved you."

"Maybe you didn't," I said.

"The truth is I never loved farming. When I met Charlotte, I saw new possibilities."

"You said you wanted to farm."

"Would it have changed anything if I told you otherwise?"

Saying yes was easy, but I doubted it was true. I had loved Morris. I never doubted I loved him, but had he asked me to leave the farm, I would have doubted his love for me.

"It's hard to remember who I was when I loved you," I said. Who had I been before I was the shaken young woman, clutching my new hat, riding the Greyhound bus back to Mansfield? I studied the face of this man.

"I spent my life believing we should have married, but I can't imagine I would have left this farm." I felt, for a moment, I betrayed myself by offering him an excuse for what he had done. "Even so, I deserved to be told. You owed me that."

He nodded and simply said, "I did owe you that."

I stood suddenly, gathered our coffee cups, and blinked away the desire to cry. Why had I done this to myself? How could I not have? I walked to the kitchen, and

Morris followed me. I picked up his gloves from the kitchen table and handed them to him. To break the silence, I asked him what Mattie and Travis had named the baby.

"Samuel."

I stepped away from him and leaned against the counter. "What?"

"Mattie wanted a family name, so I suggested what I thought Zela would have wanted. It seemed right somehow. After she left Mattie to you, I realized she wanted to hold onto our childhood, when she was happiest."

"Mattie doesn't remember, does she?" I asked, trying to remember how long it had been since I had spoken to her of my brother.

He shook his head no. Following him to the front door, I handed him his coat and scarf. He paused for a moment as if he wanted to speak.

"Dottie," he said quietly.

I shook my head. My throat tightened with sorrow. I wanted to be alone and did not need to hear any more.

"I'm glad you came," I said.

After he left, I leaned against the wall and slowly lowered myself onto the floor. I did not wipe away the quiet tears that dripped from the tip of my nose, my chin, and my eyelashes. I cried for myself. I cried for Mattie. I cried for waiting too long to cry.

Not every tree struck by lightning splintered and fell. The hickory tree in the front field had been hit twice. The first strike had severed the largest branch from the trunk. The second had flayed the bark, leaving a gash I could lean my shoulder into. If I sold a portion of the front field, I risked losing the tree to new owners who would surely chop down the damaged tree.

Within twenty-four hours of my first meeting with the real estate agent, she staked four "For Sale" signs in the front field along the road. The signs advertised five-acre lots. After calling a dozen agents in the phone book, I'd chosen her for her reasonable fees and her promise that she knew builders looking for land. On the phone we agreed to meet to discuss options and prices, but she had arrived with the "For Sale" signs in the trunk of her Oldsmobile. She wore blue jeans and a cable knit sweater that, judging by the fuchsia suit she wore in her picture, represented a gesture for rapport.

I studied the contracts under the glow of the kitchen table light while the agent spoke confidently of selling the land quickly. I wanted to tell her to leave. But I knew as I signed the paperwork to sell twenty acres that even if I sold the entire farm, I could not repay Mattie's inheritance. Mattie did not want this farm any more than Morris had. Twenty acres was not enough, but it would provide them enough money to move to California. I owed her this, at the very least.

The agent sold the first lot within a week, and I fought the impulse to yank the signs out of the soil before more of my land was carved away. When the next offer came, I could not bring myself to accept it. After a week I called the agent and promised to sign the next three contracts. I drove to the title company in Mansfield where I signed over the land. The lawyer I hired merely glanced at the documents. The paperwork was standard, nothing like my deals with my uncle.

By the third closing, I felt a small measure of relief as I signed the contract. To believe that the land was mine, I had ignored that it was Mattie's. I fought so long to own the farm, but now each sale brought me closer to admitting I never would. As I cut away one lot at a time, I walked over the muddy fields to the hickory tree and rested my hand in its gash. Getting the title from my cousin had not made this land mine. Tending it, struggling with it, loving it had.

By the middle of May, I mailed Mattie a check for twenty thousand dollars, not even a tenth of what I owed her. I also mailed her a promise that after my death she could sell the remainder of the farm and reclaim what was rightfully hers.

That afternoon I knelt beneath the hickory tree to find intact nuts. Picking through shells hulled by squirrels, I decided to tell the new owners that once this tree had won a prize for the best hickory nutmeat in Ohio. I gathered a small handful of nuts to plant when the ground thawed.

Chapter Twenty-three

In a few hours the June sun would burn off the fog, but this early in the morning it rested as heavy on the valley as a quilt, encouraging one to linger inside. The fog settled in pockets of land, creating ponds of mist. It seeped between the straight rows of corn and soybeans that had not yet thickened to hide the mechanical precision of planting.

On these summer mornings I saw the valley as I had as a young child, when my mother and I washed the breakfast dishes and watched my father and brother walk boldly into the fog. They might as well have strolled straight into the sky and through the clouds. I would not have admired or envied them more if they had.

On one of those childhood mornings I made myself a promise. I toweled off a dish and set it on the stack for my mother to lift into the cupboard and decided in the same moment that someday I would leave her side to work the farm with my father. At that time, fulfilling the promise seemed as simple as hanging the dishtowel on the metal hook by the spring-fed sink, lacing up my brother's old shoes, and running after my father and brother. The promise became a vow the day of my brother's funeral. How could I have understood then that I wanted more than to simply work this land?

A month had passed since I mailed Mattie the proceeds from the sale of the lots. The cancelled check confirmed that she received the money. I studied the small loops of her signature for some hint of emotion. Had she signed hastily in excitement or were the tight angles of her name an indication of anger? Her signature of Travis's last name appeared practiced. The swooping *S* that extended to underline her first name suggested notebook scribbling and daydreams. How many hours had she spent writing *Mattie Sullivan* on napkins, notebooks, and the dust-covered seat of the tractor? Or had I confused my desires for hers again? Was I only remembering the hours spent writing *Dottie Brubaker*? I tucked the cancelled check in the same folder where I kept the copy of the cashier's check written to Rex, a reminder to myself that I lived on borrowed land.

I did not really expect a card or a phone call from Mattie to thank me, though I jumped when the telephone rang the first few days after she cashed the check. I imagined any number of phone calls from her, from proud refusals of my attempt to meddle in her life to hesitant thanks for helping them leave for California or even furious demands for the balance of her inheritance. I had no designs for reconciliation. Reconciliation implied that we had shared love or friendship, but I had never given this to Mattie. At most we shared the memory of her mother and the memory of my attempt to raise her. I supposed we also shared a fondness for Stanley. Without him between us, we would have lacked any understanding of the other.

Before the fog cleared, I would go to the barn to continue my work replacing the barn floor. The past few weeks I ripped out rotting boards in the back right corner and laid the boards that Stanley had cut and prepared for the new floor. He had reinforced the beams of the floor to support more weight. I wanted to finish the project soon. It only reminded me that Stanley planned on finishing the project himself.

I ate the last few bites of my oatmeal covered with the strawberries I had picked with Evelyn and Retha on Saturday. Retha called as I was leaving the house to work and invited me to join them. We had not seen one another since Mr. Hilliard's funeral. I agreed to come even though I planned a full day of chores. It seemed my fondness for Mr. Hilliard would hold me to his family in spite of his death. I'd followed behind Retha and Evelyn, listening to talk of how Alice gave up her summer to substitute-teach summer school, of their church wasting too much money on a new parking lot, and of Retha's youngest boy losing his spot on the varsity football team. One could discuss these losses, and I saw the comfort in having these conversations that distracted one from real losses. I would never be one of the women of the funeral brigade. Retha and Evelyn would take their quarts of berries home to make pies and jellies, while I wanted only enough to flavor my breakfast oatmeal. Though I did not have the time or interest to make jellies and pies,

I understood then as I walked beside them that we could pick berries together just the same.

Before I left for the barn, I rinsed my bowl and took an empty Cool Whip container to fill with milk for an injured mother cat I found in the barn. I discovered her the morning I cleared out the barn to rip out the first section of the floor. A glistening trail of fresh blood led to the rusted empty waste oil barrels in the corner of the barn. I peeked behind the barrel and smelled the rot of wet straw and bat droppings. I went to the machine shed for a flashlight, and when I shone it into the corner behind the barrel, the fierce green eyes of a barn cat did not flinch. She stared at me to keep my attention from the five kittens buried into her side. I swept the flashlight over her and saw her mangled paw, clearly Frisco's doing. Every morning since, I had taken her milk or water and kept Frisco tied to a maple tree.

Two weeks earlier, as I slid the container to her and removed the empty one from the day before, I remembered reaching between barrels in the machine shed for Zela's suitcase. The cat swiped at my lingering hand, and I drew back with the realization that I had never told Mattie about her mother's suitcase. I had never told her the truth.

The next day I called the steel mill for a forwarding address for Travis, only to learn that he still worked second shift. That afternoon I sent Mattie her mother's wedding ring through insured, certified mail. I feared it would raise questions I could not answer, but when she was ready to ask questions, I would try to tell her the truth. In the same file as the signed check, I filed the notification card from the post office with Mattie's signature, confirming she had received the ring.

This foggy morning was cool. I wore a T-shirt, which I layered over with a flannel shirt and light windbreaker that I would discard in turn once my work warmed me. I carried a thermos of coffee and the cat's milk into fog that seemed to evaporate as I walked toward it. Dew darkened my boots. Some would describe the smell in the air as crisp, but to me it smelled like the absence of growth. It was too cool yet for fresh shoots of corn and beans to thicken the air with their lush, sensible smell. The bottom of my jeans and tops of my socks soaked up the dew; I needed to take an afternoon off from working in the barn to mow the grass.

A car drove slowly through the valley. The headlights made the fog seem as thick as storm clouds. I had almost reached the barn when I noticed that the car had turned onto my lane and was approaching the house. Assuming the driver was disoriented from the fog, I set the thermos and bowl of milk in the grass and walked toward the lane to offer directions.

A few boxes were strapped to the hood. A woman stepped out of the car, but the man driving kept his hands on the steering wheel, ready to leave. As I approached, I could hear a baby crying from the backseat. The woman moved away from the car but did not walk to meet me. I saw then it was Mattie. I waved but she did not wave in return.

Her face was full from weight gained in her pregnancy, which had rounded out her figure and softened the sharp angles of her adolescent body. For so long, I had seen her as the child huddled under quilts sleeping by the radiator or as the little girl too prim to step into the barn, but already she had experienced a life that eluded me.

I came up to the car and waved to Travis, who nodded but kept his hands on the wheel as if to let me know they did not plan to stay. As I neared Mattie, she stepped back from me and rested a hand on the trunk.

"This is a surprise," I said, keeping my distance. "Why don't you kids come in for some hot coffee?"

"We have a long drive ahead of us today. We're hoping to get to St. Louis by this evening."

"Did you send a moving truck ahead of you?"

"We sold our used furniture. No sense taking it across country."

The baby had stopped crying. The car was still running, but Travis leaned over the front seat and danced a stuffed dog above the baby. "Is he close to three months now?"

Mattie nodded. "We've got him settled in the back. It'll be too hard to get him out for you to hold him." She said it quickly, as if she had practiced these words all the way to the farm. I stopped myself from saying I hadn't asked to hold him, because in truth I hoped that I could.

"Did you get breakfast before you got on the road? I've got biscuits made and could fix eggs in a minute."

"We hadn't planned on stopping long. I promised Travis we'd get back on the road in a few minutes." Mattie leaned back against the car and crossed her arms. She studied me and then asked, "How did you get my mother's ring?"

"This isn't a conversation to have in the middle of the lane. You should come in."

"Why wasn't she wearing it when she died?"

I could tell her any number of truths or simply say I didn't know why, which was the closest to the truth but not entirely honest. For all these years, Morris and I hid Zela's story from the newspaper and from our neighbors. The uncertainty of her mother's actions that night would only hurt Mattie. How could Mattie understand, when I, who had known Zela since childhood, did not?

"I found it in a suitcase hidden in my shed after she died. I believe your mother meant to leave your father that night. She had you stay with me so she could tell him their marriage was over. Her suitcase was full of clothes and so was yours. She packed for more than one night for both of you."

Mattie turned away from me and stared toward the machine shed. Travis shook a rattle, trying to quiet the whimpering baby. He exaggerated a smile for the baby and then a look of surprise.

"She didn't intend for me to grow up here?" she asked.

"I don't know what she planned. Sometimes I think she wanted both of you to stay here because it reminded her of better times. I know she didn't want you to grow up without her."

The baby's whimpers escalated into crying that Travis tried to shush. He dug in a bag near the baby. Mattie glanced toward the backseat and said, "I knew it was a lie. I never believed my mother wanted you to raise me."

"She was my oldest and closest friend. She named me in her will," I said softly to her and to myself.

As the baby's cries turned to screams, Travis took the baby from the backseat into the front seat. He rolled down the window and yelled, "He does better when we're driving."

"We'll leave in a minute," Mattie called back, without looking away from me, and then she said, "If you'd believed my mother wanted you to raise me, you would have shown me the ring years ago."

I could only nod. I owed her that. Travis got out of the car and paced a few yards, trying to quiet the baby.

"You're right," I finally said. I realized we might not talk again. "I thought I raised you out of love for your mother. But I should have raised you because I loved you as a daughter. I'm sorry."

"We have to go," she said, as if she hadn't heard me. I had not meant to foist an apology on her. I did not want her to feel she owed me a reply.

"May I see him?" I asked.

Travis walked down the lane with the baby and was watching, through the fog, two construction trucks driving onto the cleared lot where they would build the first house on the front field. They had already dug out the basement and poured the foundation. A backhoe beeped as it reversed to the trenches they had dug the day before to lay the plumbing. The baby quieted for a moment as Travis bounced him slightly. The backhoe dug into soil that yielded a lush corn crop the year before.

Mattie watched them and then said suddenly, "There was a Samuel in your family."

"My brother. Your mother and uncle loved him like a brother."

Mattie said quietly, "I can't get away from this place."

Another truck arrived with men sitting in the truck bed. The backhoe groaned as the operator brought it to a stop. He climbed down and joined the other workmen. "What are you working on now?" she asked.

"They don't work for me. They're building on the lots I sold."

"They're tearing up the front field."

I nodded. "It was the best for building. I knew it would sell faster than the others."

"So that's where you got the money."

"You don't need to concern yourself with that. I owed you that money."

"You'll hate having neighbors that close."

"Not unless they put up scarecrows in their three-row gardens."

"How many acres did you sell?"

When I told her twenty, she looked at me quickly, appearing more shocked than when I told her I was sorry. She narrowed her eyes for a moment as she always did before she argued with me, then she cocked her head with a realization. These expressions were so familiar to me. It surprised me to recognize that, for all our misunderstandings, we had spent ten years together. She walked over to Travis and took Samuel from him. She tucked a blanket around his feet and then walked back to me. "This is Samuel."

She handed him to me. His face puckered into full screams. I held him upright and faced the woods my brother had loved. He still cried. I turned back toward the machines and tried to buoy him as Travis had. "You cried like this," I told her, "when your mother visited me. The only thing that quieted you was when she held you close to her with one arm and swung you back and forth." I balanced Samuel the way Zela had held Mattie. With my arm firmly under his stomach, I cradled him near me and slowly rocked him. Gradually he stopped crying. I felt an ache as I realized they would leave.

"He reminds me of you," I said.

"You knew we'd use the money to go to California."

"It's where you belong."

"You said I belonged here."

"That's what I wanted."

Travis came up to us and lightly touched Mattie's back. "We're going to get in late tonight."

"One minute," she said. "He's calming down."

Travis went to the car and opened the back passenger-side door. Mattie held out her arms and took Samuel from me, and I followed her to the car. She turned toward me before she laid Samuel in a nest of blankets in the backseat. I wanted to hug her, but she kept her distance.

"I'll send you a postcard when we get to California," she said.

"I'd like that."

Travis got in the car, and the Datsun sputtered to a start. I held my hand on the door to feel useful as she leaned in and tucked the blankets around Samuel. Pillows filled the floor of the passenger side so that he would not roll out of the small pocket in the blankets. Mattie reached past the baby behind Travis's seat and jimmied out a vase held in place by books on photography and darkrooms.

The vase was filled with pebbles and a plant with knobby-fingered roots that conformed to the sides of the vase. "I should leave this with you. You can make anything grow. This was my attempt to grow something indoors, but it keeps tipping over every time Travis goes around a curve. It should've bloomed by now." As she handed it to me, she patted my arm awkwardly.

"I'll take good care of it," I said.

She opened her door. "Mattie," I said suddenly. I cleared my throat. It was harder to say a second time. "I don't expect you to say anything in return, but I want to know you've heard me. I worked so hard to run this farm that I never loved you as I should have."

Mattie looked at the ground and kicked a few stones. It reminded me of the first morning we had walked to the barn in the snow, and she had kicked her own path next to mine. This was what I should have allowed in her. This was what I should have loved in her.

"I'll write when we get to California," she said as she got into the car. Travis rolled down the window and waved as I waved to them. As they left the lane he honked the horn once, and they were gone.

Retha would not loan me her flower book to identify the plant with roots that stuck like twigs into water. She insisted it would save time if I drove to her house and let her see it. After she had pronounced it an amaryllis, she laughed at me for filling a flowerpot and transferring the flower to soil. "This doesn't seem your type of flower, Dottie," she said as she searched under her kitchen sink for what she called a bulb forcer. After agreeing to sit for a glass of sun tea, I took home the bulb forcer, shaped like an hourglass. As instructed, I filled half of the vase with water and rested the bulb on the slight pinch in the glass. I positioned it on my nightstand next to my bed to receive the early morning light.

Within days, three pods, heavy with the promise of blossoms, reached toward my bedroom window. Each night I tilted back the stem and filled the vase with water. Each day I checked the mailbox for Mattie's postcard. I worked on the barn floor and then by late afternoon I walked to the end of the lane to check the box.

After two weeks, a card finally came. It was cartoonish with garish oranges, yellows, and reds that said, "Greetings from California." Mattie had simply written, "We're here! Travis starts classes in August. Samuel loves the ocean. Love, Mattie." I propped the card against the vase so that when I woke in the morning I looked first at the card and then at the amaryllis. Instead of studying her signature, I examined how she had written *love*. Presumably she had written it out of habit, but I kept the card turned so I could see it when I woke.

The day after I finished flooring the right side of the barn, I woke late, my knees aching from hours of kneeling forward to hammer the boards in place. The hazy light of morning surprised me with its brightness. I always woke to the light of dawn, not morning. I chided myself for losing an hour in bed, but then I saw the amaryllis.

A white, five-pointed blossom had opened in morning's first light. The amaryllis had bloomed without soil. I settled under the covers and marveled at the translucent bloom glowing with the light of the sun. My body, warm with sleep, relaxed in the pale reflective light of this flower. Without a thought of the day to come, I watched the petals take on the brightness of daylight as time passed.

I imagined finding Mattie's old Brownie camera to take pictures of the bloom as she would have. A cluster of viny roots woven through water and rocks. A rectangle of sunlight on a leaf. A single white petal.

I was awed by this flower. My cornfields afforded me greater pride in their promise, and my wheat fields, which glowed orange at sunrise, astonished me in their beauty, but of all that I had ever grown, this amaryllis blossom, which extended its roots into water rather than anchoring in soil, had the most grace.

Acknowledgments

I am deeply indebted to Frank, Beth, and Tom Baumberger, whose Ohio farm inspired this book's setting and who educated me on everything from farming practices to driving a tractor. I would also like to express my gratitude to the following: Lawrence and Helen Vincent, Clarissa McQuade, Viola Eaton, Val Margot, and Joann Williams for historical and farming details; Peggy at Malabar Farm for answering questions alongside morning chores; the archivists at the Sherman Room at the Mansfield/Richland County Public Library; my invaluable assistant Leigh Ann Ruggiero; and my colleague and friend David Wright for titles and for cheering me on.

I would like to thank my editors: Gretchen Jaeger for her commitment to this book and for knowing what it needed and Lil Copan for her patience, humor, and keen eye. I am forever grateful to Sheri Reynolds for seeing the possibility of this book in a short story and Janet Peery for her surpassing insight that rescued an early draft and her generous encouragement.

I thank my family for their unwavering support, especially my mother, Jan McQuade, for listening to my earliest stories on long walks and my father, Brian McQuade, for waking me at sunrise to show me the land of his childhood as he loves it best. Most of all, I thank my husband, Chris, who made this novel possible.

An Interview *with* Nicole Mazzarella on Her Novel *This Heavy Silence*

Interviewer: Everyone has someone like Dottie in their lives. Most people wouldn't be brave enough to explore a character who isn't initially likeable, but whose interior struggle the reader sees and gradually has great compassion for. How did you decide to take this sort of risk in fiction?

NM: Dottie first appeared in one of my short stories as a minor character who was jilted by her fiancé. The second time I wrote about Dottie she was an eight-year-old at her brother's funeral. So I first encountered Dottie as a young woman full of desire and as a child desperate for her father's attention. It is sometimes easier to have compassion for someone in the midst of those situations than for someone embittered by those experiences.

I wondered who Dottie would become following these events, and this led to a draft of the novel that spanned seventy years of Dottie's life. Dottie's responses to these losses shaped the writing of every scene that followed. This does not mean that I found it easy to write Dottie. In fact, I resisted writing many scenes, because I cared equally for Mattie and Stanley. But then I would realize that given Dottie's choices, the scene could be written only one way. Once I recognized the woman who Dottie had become, I hoped that readers would grow to understand her, even if they disagreed with her. It did feel like a risk at times. Yet I reread the books that challenge or enlarge my understanding of others, and I can only hope to do the same.

Interviewer: Landscape not only informs the writing, but envelops the entire book, as though landscape were a protagonist in the book. Is this your own experience with landscape, or did you try to inhabit someone else's understanding of how landscape informs a farmer like Dottie?

NM: Toni Morrison counsels novelists to write the books they want to read. While I tried to heed this advice, I also initially wrote this novel where I wanted to dwell imaginatively. I'm a functioning suburbanite, but I breathe easier in the landscape where I set the novel. Living outside of Ohio when I began the novel, I discovered that many people are not familiar with this landscape. They envision the flatlands of the Midwest, rather than the lush, glacial-hewn valleys in areas like Pleasant Valley in Lucas, Ohio. As I wrote I spread photographs of this valley across my desk and imagined driving the dusty lane to Dottie's house and sitting on her front porch to hear her story. So each day I returned to this landscape where I am most at home.

The landscape as a protagonist in the novel simply reflects my experience that where we live is more than a backdrop for our lives. I moved three times during the four years of writing the novel; each move reminded me how our environment alters us. I'm most at home in a place where I kick off muddied shoes at the end of the day.

Interviewer: You mentioned photographs of the valley that inspired the novel. How familiar were you with this setting before you began writing the novel?

NM: It was not only my familiarity with but also my love of this area of Ohio that led me to set the novel there. While the events and characters are fictional, you can visit the farm that inspired this novel: Maplewood Farm in Lucas, Ohio. In fact I visit it nearly every time I return to Ohio. My great-aunt and uncle still own this farm where my grandmother grew up. As a child we took many Sunday drives through Pleasant Valley as my father told me stories about his childhood in this valley.

Topics for Contemplation

or Group Discussion

To Love and Lose Another

"An oak tree could stand for two hundred years. . . .
Long enough to hold tree houses and swings
that would rot and fall from them like a slow autumn.
Long enough to forget they could fall."

1. How did you feel when Stanley left? Were you disappointed that he did not return? What do you think influenced his decision to leave?
2. "Winter, like grieving, was a succession of false endings" (page 57). How does Dottie grieve the various losses she has experienced? How does this change throughout the course of the novel? How did you feel when she finally cries for herself, for Mattie, and for "waiting too long to cry"?
3. The first-person perspective that the novel uses allows readers to see a side of Dottie hidden from most people. For example, when Stanley lingers in the kitchen one evening, she considers "[asking] him to put his arms around [her]," but instead "stepped back, distrusting [her] desire . . ." (page 176). In which other scenes do we observe Dottie's actions conflicting with her thoughts and emotions? How would her life differ if she revealed these thoughts and emotions? Also given the first-person perspective, are there places when you mistrust Dottie's own perception of events?
4. Dottie's work often symbolizes the state of her emotional life. How does the birthing scene in Chapter Two parallel Mattie's entrance into her life? How does the scene of Stanley and Dottie unearthing rocks in Chapter Seventeen parallel their relationship?

To Become A Mother

"I envied mothers who had nine months to grow accustomed to the weight of a child and whose hollowed wombs created an instinct to remember their children."

5. How did you feel when Dottie adopted Mattie? Why? What are the various reasons behind Dottie's agreeing to raise Mattie? Does Dottie fully understand her motivations?
6. How does Dottie's gender influence her community's expectations of how she should raise Mattie? How are her deficiencies as a mother accentuated by her gender? Are the women in the community justified in encouraging Dottie to give Mattie to her former fiancé?
7. When the novel shifts forward a decade, what subtle changes do you notice in Dottie? How has raising Mattie changed her?
8. Three months after Mattie leaves, Dottie says that Mattie has become too much like her (page 222). Does Mattie share any similarities with Dottie? How do you think Mattie would respond to this comparison?
9. Did it seem realistic that Mattie moved but still lived in a nearby town? How would you have responded if you were Mattie?
10. The actions of parents influence many generations in *This Heavy Silence.* Dottie's grandfather's decision to leave the farm to his eldest son has repercussions for many generations. How do patterns in parent/child relationships continue throughout the novel?
11. Dottie inherits her mother's "cadenced work ethic" (page 6) and learns from her father that "labor was the appropriate response to grief, that sorrow and loneliness were fruitless emotions. They did not give me the strength to press into the day and work to exhaustion. They would not yield anything I could point to and be proud of" (page 229). How do you think it influences someone to be raised by parents who have this view of work?

To Live in a Place of Silences

"Her silence encouraged my silence."

12. The title *This Heavy Silence* draws our attention to the various silences in the novel. Which silence caused the greatest harm and to whom? What situations led characters to respond with silence? How might their relationships have changed if they risked breaking this silence? How have you observed the effects of silences within your own family or friendships?
13. Dottie says, "The heaviness of the silence that followed the prayers felt as immense as God. I couldn't say what I expected to hear. But the silence settled on me like an accusation, and in those moments I believed there was a God." Why might Dottie hear the silence as an accusation? What has caused Dottie to trust and mistrust God?
14. The farm is as vivid a character as any in the novel. How does Dottie's relationship with the farm compare to her relationship with people? How does the writer convey the setting through description and also through dialogue and characters?
15. When Rex asks Dottie what she promised her father that ties her to the land, she replies, "No promise is stronger than one we make with ourselves" (page 89). Why does Dottie farm her family's land? Do you think vows to others or to ourselves control us more?

To Know Another

"No one outside the valley would understand a woman waving a rifle for three hundred acres."

16. What was your first impression of Dottie? How did your view of her change? If you could have a conversation with Dottie, what would you say to her?

17. Which character do you relate to most? Though Dottie comes across as a distant character, can you relate to her on some level?
18. Which characters remind you most of someone you know? Have you ever known someone like Dottie?
19. In the final scene, Dottie imagines how Mattie would photograph the amaryllis and rests in awe of this flower. How is this flower different from everything she has ever grown? Given the changes she experiences at the end of the novel, what are your hopes for Dottie?

As You Read

Suggestions for Discussion Groups

The Comfort of Food

The "funeral brigade" arrives after Zela's death to stock Dottie's refrigerator with meals. They bring food associated with comfort: macaroni and cheese, venison chili, and corn muffins. Make a menu of the food that brings your discussion group the most comfort and share this meal with your group as you discuss *This Heavy Silence.*

"Tobacco for a Rainy Day"

Dottie's father kept boots with good soles and magazines to read. What odd item do you have stashed in the back of a closet? Bring the object and a story to share with your discussion group. Then discuss how Dottie has been influenced by this heritage of holding onto things (the hickory tree in the middle of the front field, her grandfather's corn drill behind the barn, her father's leaf collection).

"Greetings from California"

The novel ends with a postcard from Mattie. What would you say to Dottie in a postcard? Write a postcard and bring it to share with your discussion group.

Discussions with the Author

Occasionally Nicole Mazzarella enjoys meeting with book clubs. Please contact Paraclete Press (www.paracletepress.com) for the author's travel schedule and the possibility of inviting her to join your discussion. For more information on the novel and the author, visit www.nicolemazzarella.com.

About Paraclete Press

Who We Are

Paraclete Press is an ecumenical publisher of books and recordings on Christian spirituality. Our publishing represents a full expression of Christian belief and practice—from Catholic to Evangelical, from Protestant to Orthodox.

Paraclete Press is the publishing arm of the Community of Jesus, an ecumenical monastic community in the Benedictine tradition. As such, we are uniquely positioned in the marketplace without connection to a large corporation and with informal relationships to many branches and denominations of faith.

We like it best when people buy our books from booksellers, our partners in successfully reaching as wide an audience as possible.

What We Are Doing

Books

Paraclete Press publishes books that show the richness and depth of what it means to be Christian. Although Benedictine spirituality is at the heart of all that we do, we publish books that reflect the Christian experience across many cultures, time periods, and houses of worship.

We publish books that nourish the vibrant life of the church and its people—books about spiritual practice, formation, history, ideas, and customs.

We have several different series of books within Paraclete Press, including the bestselling Living Library series of modernized classic texts; A Voice from the Monastery—giving voice to men and women monastics about what it means to live a spiritual life today; award-winning literary faith fiction; and books that explore Judaism and Islam and discover how these faiths inform Christian thought and practice.

Recordings

From Gregorian chant to contemporary American choral works, our music recordings celebrate the richness of sacred choral music through the centuries. Paraclete is proud to distribute the recordings of the internationally acclaimed choir Gloriæ Dei Cantores, who have been praised for their "rapt and fathomless spiritual intensity" by *American Record Guide,* and the Gloriæ Dei Cantores Schola, which specializes in the study and performance of Gregorian chant. Paraclete is also the exclusive North American distributor of the recordings of the Monastic Choir of St. Peter's Abbey in Solesmes, France, long considered to be a leading authority on Gregorian chant performance.